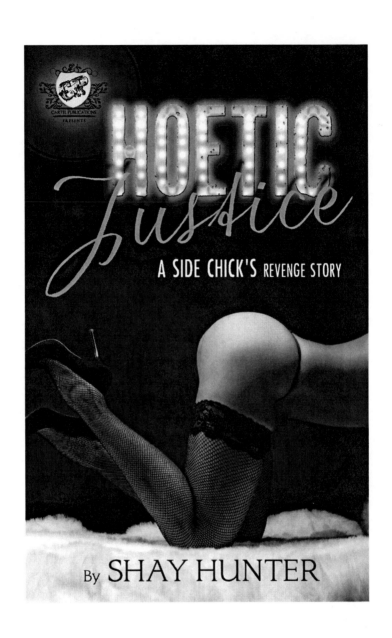

HOETIC Justice

A SIDE CHICK'S REVENGE STORY

By SHAY HUNTER

By Shay Hunter

ARE YOU ON OUR EMAIL LIST?

SIGN UP ON OUR WEBSITE

www.thecartelpublications.com

OR TEXT THE WORD:

CARTELBOOKS TO 22828

FOR PRIZES, CONTESTS, ETC.

4   *By Shay Hunter*

WWW.THECARTELPUBLICATIONS.COM

Hoetic Justice   5

By Shay Hunter

HOETIC JUSTICE

By

Shay Hunter

Library of Congress Control Number: 2014951120

ISBN 10: 0996099298

ISBN 13: 978-0996099295

Cover Design: Davida Baldwin www.oddballdsgn.com
Editor(s): T. Styles, C. Wash, S. Ward
www.thecartelpublications.com
First Edition
Printed in the United States of America

8   *By Shay Hunter*

What's Up Fam,

I'ma keep this one short and sweet so you can jump right into this new shit Shay is bringing you. "Hoetic Justice" is a live one! It jumps right into the middle of the action and before you know it, you're on the last page lost wondering where the time went. We truly hope you enjoy it as much as we did.

Keeping in line with tradition, we want to give respect to a vet or trailblazer paving the way. With that said we would like to recognize:

Julie Ojeda Nin

Julie is the veteran author of the novels, "Friends 'Til The End" and "Friends 'Til The End II". In this series, Julie paints a vivid picture of the streets of New York, the good and the ugly, through the life of a teenage girl named Jessie. This series is live and Julie is one of the sweetest people you would ever want to meet. If you have not already done so, please make sure you check out her work. You won't be disappointed.

Aight, get to it. I'll get at you in the next novel.

Be Easy!

Charisse "C. Wash" Washington

Vice President

The Cartel Publications

www.thecartelpublications.com

www.facebook.com/publishercwash

Instagram: publishercwash

www.twitter.com/cartelbooks

www.facebook.com/cartelpublications

Follow us on Instagram: Cartelpublications

By Shay Hunter

#HoeticJustice

PROLOGUE

It was my mission to scratch as much makeup and skin off her pretty face as possible. I succeeded too. Because when I finished wind milling she was wearing pink tiger stripes on her forehead and cheeks and I was just getting started.

I guess when she stepped to me she hadn't expected me to be so angry. She seemed scared by my reaction and tried to step away but I yanked her by her hair forcing her back into my space. I wasn't done with her just yet. I didn't want a fight at first but there was so much left to say. She was the cause of my emotional pain and now I wanted her to feel as bad as I did.

When she first walked up on me things weren't violent. I pointed a stiff finger in her face and we had words. I tried my best to land as much spit on her nose as possible as I screamed each word I spoke. The

By Shay Hunter

sensation I felt as I called her everything but a child of God gave me a tingling feeling I couldn't explain.

I was sick of this bitch coming at me like I was the one who stepped up on myself at a Ravens football game two years ago and asked for my own number. I was sick of this bitch coming at me like I was the one who busted a nut inside of myself so many times I had five abortions before finally keeping one. And I was sick of this bitch acting like I was holding Devin hostage when he was the one gripping me up while whispering in my ear that he didn't want to ever let me go. Bitch please.

At the end of the day he wanted both of us and as far as I was concerned I didn't see a problem with it. Just as long as he didn't treat me any different from his wife I was winning all the way around. She was the one trying to stop the program. If she thought calling my phone all hours of the night with her empty ass threats would run me off she had another thing coming. She was gonna have to accept me just like I had to accept her or risk losing him altogether.

I was just about to tell her how good it felt the last time Devin and I fucked when suddenly I felt a cool stinging sensation in my lower belly. When I looked down to see what caused the pain, my eyes widened when I saw her easing a silver blade doused with blood from my body.

With wide eyes I stumbled away from her and fell back into the rack of potato chips. Suddenly I was looking up at the grungy ceiling. The pain was getting worse and I could feel warm blood oozing from the wound and toward my back.

I didn't think things would get this bad. I never thought she'd go this far. Lately we fought so much that I talked to her more than I did Devin. I guess I should've known how much she cared about him because I felt the same way.

At first it was all about the money and sex but soon things changed. I caught feelings.

But at the end of the day I was the side chick and he was her husband.

CHAPTER ONE

CLEVERLY

BALTIMORE MARYLAND

I can't believe I'm sitting on my knees, on my sofa, looking out the window like a fucking kid. I was waiting on my bum ass baby's father to come get our child. Devin told me he'd be here five hours ago and I was supposed to be at the party right now shaking my ass with the rest of my friends.

But no.

Thanks to this nigga I was looking into the street with our son Village on my hip, waiting for him to show up. My son's soggy pamper felt like warm gel against my side but I don't feel like changing him right now. If Devin would've been here that would be his job.

By Shay Hunter

This shit is so unfair!

When I met Devin two years ago at a Ravens football game I knew we would be connected forever in some kind of way. His dark chocolate skin and smooth baldhead made me grin every time I thought about him or was in his presence. It wasn't just how he looked but what he did when he was around me. Money wasn't a thing for him and I always felt like a queen.

My friends and me were in the nosebleed section and he had someone follow me from the concession stand back to our seats. Later I would find out that his name was Prize, one of Devin's best friends. "What you ladies doing this far up?" he asked looking at the three of us.

"Watching the game just like you," I responded.

"Why don't you hang out with me and my friends in the end zone?" Prize said. "If nothing else you'll be able to see better."

I didn't see a problem with it so my bitches and me walked all the way down to seats so good it felt like I was one of the players. After my friends took a seat and Prize and Mace moved over there was only one available spot left...next to Devin.

The moment I laid eyes on him I knew he was for me. His skin tone matched mine and his white teeth blinged so brightly I had to turn away. We clicked so hard that when I looked up the Ravens had beaten the Patriots and we didn't even know what happened. We had so much in common. He was a gamer just like me. He lived in Baltimore and he liked to drink as much as I did.

I loved everything about him except his wedding ring, which he didn't take off. "I'm feeling you,

18   *By Shay Hunter*

Clever," he said as I rode shotgun in his BMW. "But I'm married and I'm not going to lie to you and say that I'm unhappy. Right now my wife is everything I want in a woman."

"Then why you want me?" I asked.

"Because I want more," he paused. "Add the fact that I'm bored. And I'm a nigga who wants a little something different. Can you get with that?"

I answered his question by hanging around for two years, getting multiple abortions because he didn't want to pull out of my pussy and believing him when he said despite not having the ring that I was number one.

I hadn't always been the type of chick who would play these games. At 26 years old I know I'm putting myself in a bad predicament. But I fell in love before with a man who I thought was all mine only to learn he wasn't. His name was Ranch Murphy and we were high school sweethearts. There was a Facebook page that we didn't create in high school that showed our love. Everyone I went to school with said the same thing, that they wanted the relationship Clever and Ranch had.

We were envied.

When we got out of high school we got our first apartment. He went to college for engineering and I remained unemployed so I could take care of him. For two years things were sweet and then he came into the bathroom while I was taking a bath one day and said, "I found somebody else, Clever. But we can still be friends."

Even now it's hard to describe the pain I was in. Ranch wasn't a part of my world, he *was* my world. I begged him the entire night to reconsider but he wasn't hearing me. I knew then that he had fallen in love with her a long time ago. This wasn't a fly by night situation. I was right when I found out he married Ashanti Mercer, a chick in my biology class from high school. She was the same bitch who created the Facebook page showing pics of the cutest couple. She didn't think our relationship was cute, she wanted our relationship and she got it.

Ranch moved out the next day after he told me he was in love with another chick and I made up my mind that it would never happen again. I didn't want a man of my own. I wanted everybody else's and no man was off limits...and that included married men.

"I can't believe you still looking out that fucking window," my friend Vanessa said. "The nigga not coming, Clever. Why you playing yourself soft?"

Irritated with her I released the thick black curtain and flopped down on the sofa. I placed my son Village next to me and he picked up his bottle halfway filled with apple juice and stuffed the nipple in his mouth. It produced the sound of air and juice being sucked in at the same time. "First off I'm not playing myself like anything. If he says he coming he coming."

Sitting on my brown recliner she threw her head back and shook her head. The twist-out hairstyle she sported in her natural mane produced large brown curls that spilled over her lightface. "When you gonna realize the nigga don't want you?" she knocked a thick wad of hair from her eye. "The only thing he good for is dick. Nothing else and nothing more."

"You don't know what you talking about."

"Please don't tell me you fell in love with him," she said. "When you know how niggas are. The dude is married, Clever! Wake up!"

"What's wrong with a married nigga?" My other friend, Tracy, asked as she strutted out of my kitchen holding a jug of apple juice. When she reached the couch she sat it on the table and grabbed Village's baby bottle.

"Nothing if you aren't in love with them. So don't even come for me," Vanessa said.

"I'm serious. Why should I show respect to a ring or a marriage certificate if the dude don't?" Tracy continued. "The only question you should be asking is this." She looked over at me. "Clever, are you going with us to the club or not?" she filled his bottle and handed it back to him. "Because I got a lot of shit on my mind that only dick can take care of."

"I'm trying but what else can I do? Devin promised to have his mother watch Village and I was waiting for that break." I paused. "Ya'll know I can't go unless he gets his son," I turned around and pushed the curtain again hoping to see the Range Rover sign on his black truck. When he wasn't there I released it and shook my head. "Let me call him again."

Both of them sighed.

"Don't call him back," Vanessa said waving her hand. "Devin's ass is not about to come get no baby on a Saturday night. Just so you can go ripping and running the streets. Chile, please!"

"Yeah, why don't you call your Aunt Annette," Tracy said as she plopped down on a plastic chair next to the couch. She pulled out a makeup mirror and eased a soft pink blush over her chocolate skin before smoothing her fine hair with her hand. "She'll watch him."

"I know she'll watch him," I sighed. "But it's time that Devin starts getting his child more. Plus I want him to be around his other grandmother and stuff."

Vanessa giggled. "Keep it real, Clever. All you want to do is have Rain's ass pop up over her mother-in-law's house and have to explain what she's doing with a baby. Bitch, don't try to run game on me."

"It ain't about that," I said seriously. "It's about what I said. Knowing both sides of his family will be good for my son. Village knows mine; he should know Devin's too. I ain't make this baby on my own you know?"

"Actually you did," Vanessa responded. "You got pregnant and carried him on your own. You were even alone when you gave birth to him. Devin told you a million times he didn't sign up for no kid and you didn't listen. Bet you hear him now though."

My eyes squinted as I looked over at her. Out of the three of us Vanessa was the main one who thought just because she saw Prize, one of Devin's friends, more than I saw Devin, or Tracy saw Mace that she was better than us. The entire thing was comical because at the end of the day not one of our dudes ever stayed long enough to let the sun rise catch them out. We were all side chicks no matter how they spun it.

"Bitch, if you think I made this boy by myself you dumber than I thought. Furthermore I know I can call my aunt but I'm tired of relying on her. She got a life too."

"Which she would gladly give up for five dollars a piece from us and a pack of Newport's," Vanessa responded. "So instead of wasting time on Devin's baldheaded ass how 'bout we put the ends together and hit her up."

"Yeah, bitch. The night is still young," Tracy said.

I was leaning against the bar, holding my fourth glass of berry Ciroc, courtesy of one of the many guys who thought I was so sexy. At 5'5 with skin the color of dark sweet chocolate I didn't have a problem pulling a

By Shay Hunter

man. It always fucked my head up when dark-skinned chicks said it was hard to get a guy because I could never beat them off. Maybe it was the fat ass or the cute face but something about me was obviously appealing.

When my drink was done I slammed the glass on the bar and ran my hand down the side of the tight blue jeans I wore. Then I looked down at the white top I was sporting hoping I was showing cleavage instead of my full breasts.

Every time I thought about Devin I would accept another drink and now I was finding it hard to stand up straight. I was going to have to get my mind off him or my night would be ruined. After dancing with a few dudes I chose the one who looked most promising. His name was Lotus and he was all right on the eyes. He was a little louder than I liked my men but he was dressed nice and didn't mind spending money on my friends and me.

"So what's up, sexy?" Lotus said as he screamed down at me to be heard over the music. "I've been trying to get at you all night. You and your friends coming to VIP with me and my boys or what?" He repositioned the gold lion medallion that fell against his black t-shirt. I must not have answer him fast enough because he picked up the empty glass I was drinking from off the bar and said, "You'll never go dry if you come with me."

I didn't mean to take so long to answer. Once again my thoughts rolled on Devin and what he was doing. I missed him so much and hated myself for catching feelings but it was too late.

"Bitch, are we going or what?" Tracy asked walking up behind me. She didn't care that old boy was standing there. "I ain't trying to spend my money if I don't have to. Let's roll with 'em."

"I'm not trying to grab my wallet either, Clever," Vanessa said. "What we gonna do?"

I looked up at Lotus and said, "If you pouring we drinking."

We were in VIP for an hour and Lotus was showing me a lot of attention. It felt good but he wasn't who I wanted to be with. I wanted Devin and it was fucking my head up. I know what kind of girl I am. I'm the one who makes niggas happy. I'm not supposed to get serious and I'm not supposed to want more than a few dollars and an hour of quality time. But when I was with Devin the days just seemed to fly by and I could never get enough of him. I wanted him for myself but I knew my vision was a fairytale.

After an hour the more time I spent with Lotus the angrier I got with Devin. He hadn't bothered to call my phone once. He stood me up and gave me his ass to kiss. It's like he doesn't give a fuck despite what he says in my ear when my pussy juice is spilling all over him.

I feel bad for my present company. Lotus was making me feel like I could be the one if I wanted. Each time my cup emptied he'd fill it up and looked at me like he'd been waiting all of his life. I might be the side chick but I'm a top notch one. And if Devin wanted to play me like I didn't matter than I guess it is what it is.

While Lotus had his arm draped over the back of my chair I pulled out my cell phone and texted Devin.

Lose my number bitch! I'm done.

By Shay Hunter

CHAPTER TWO
DEVIN
WASHINGTON DC

I didn't feel like this crying shit my wife was doing right now. I was standing in the middle of my bedroom looking down at my wife who was crying for no reason at all. When we first got together I couldn't stand to see a tear fall from her beautiful chocolate face but now I didn't give a fuck. She acted like every time I left the house I was fucking another bitch. Yeah I might've hit my side chick off every now and again but for the most part I was about that money. Somewhere along the line my wife changed and I ain't like it at all.

I met her in a bookstore when I was buying another chick, who was sitting in my car at the time, an urban

Hoetic Justice   31

book. When I reached the counter Rain was arguing with the cashier about a credit she should have on an account. I couldn't make out the first things she was saying because I was so busy focusing on her bubble ass. Her waist was so tiny that I was surprised she could even drag that thing around. But when I removed my eyes off her cheeks I zeroed in on the conversation.

"I'm saying, I've been in here every day for the last month," Rain yelled. "Finally the grant agency answered me." She slammed a piece of paper on the counter. "And here is the copy of the check. The physical copy is on the way. They told me all I had to do was show you this and I should be good for the credit I need to buy my books right now."

"I understand, ma'am," the cashier jabbed the keyboard a few times and looked at the screen." But the credit does not reflect on your account just yet. There's nothing I can do."

"But I need my fucking—"

"Aye...how much is the balance?" I asked standing behind Rain.

"Eight hundred dollars," the cashier said. The cashier looked as if she was surprised I even asked.

I reached in my pocket and handed her eight hundred dollar bills and a twenty. Most chicks would be grateful but Rain said, "Why you do that shit? You don't even know me."

I paid for the book I had for my shawty who was waiting in my car, along with hers and said, "So you not going to thank me? Even though you can buy new books and you'll have a credit on your account later?"

"Nigga, take your drug dealing ass and your money and get the fuck up out my face. I'm about my education, not about fucking with some dope boy who gonna be dead in less than a month."

She was talking all that fly shit but when night fell she was sitting on top of my dick, raw, telling me how much she liked me from jump. And that she knew I had many bitches on my roster. The books I bought her lay in the seat next to us. She hadn't even cracked them open. I was sliding in and out of her like she belonged to me.

Even though I hit the first day I still liked her. She was serious about school and she had a dream I could stand behind. She wanted to be a doctor and since I wasn't the college type dude it felt good being able to say that I helped her get a degree. So whatever tuition grants didn't cover I picked them up. Before long I realized that although she was not as wild as the chicks I fucked from time to time, she was wifey material and that meant a lot to me. The deal was solidified when I brought her to my mother, who I'm very close with, and she said she was a keeper. With my mother's approval I asked Rain Donavon to change her last name to Yokes and be my wife.

She accepted.

For the first year she tried her best to do the fun shit I liked and go to school at the same time. I liked video games and she learned to play. I liked smoking weed during the week and she puffed every time I passed. I liked to drink on the weekends and go see the strippers and she was always by my side. But she was also tired the next morning when she went to school and her work suffered. So I stopped asking her out because I wanted her to get her degree. I loved my wife and nothing was more important than seeing her dream realized. I was a hood nigga and if I wanted a hood bitch as a wife I would not have married her.

She was disappointed that we couldn't spend as much time together and I told her not to be. I was going to ride with her even if she couldn't be my best friend. But it didn't stop the need I had to do fun shit when I wasn't hustling. Dope boy work was hard and I liked to make sure playtime was just as hard.

That's where a good side bitch came in.

"Rain, why you acting like this?" I asked squeezing her shoulders. "I'm not cheating on you, baby. You know that." Two strands of snot oozed out of her nose and rolled toward her upper lip. I wiped it away and put it on her shirt on the sly when I gripped her again. "You know I'm not about that shit. Fuck I look like cheating on you when you give me everything I want?"

She sniffled a few times and wiped her tears away. "Then why are you always leaving the house? It seems like you're gone more times than you're here, Devin! You act like you not even married."

When I felt my phone vibrating in my pocket I grew angrier with her although I tried to hide it. Earlier I got a text from Clever saying she was done with me and to lose her number. That fucked my head up because there wasn't a bitch I fucked who had as wet a pussy as she did. She was also crazy sexy. Next to my wife nobody could fuck with her in the looks department and I appreciated her for keeping her body tight. I'm a sucker for dark skin chicks with big asses and small titties and Clever is just what I ordered.

But, there were two things I didn't like about Clever. First she had a baby I begged her not to have. She knew I was married. What the fuck was she thinking? Any other time I got her pregnant she would go to Planned Parenthood on Howard Street and have an abortion but this time it was different. She took my money, claimed she was going and nine months later I had a son.

We had a fall out over that shit too and for her entire pregnancy I didn't talk to her. But the moment I saw my kid there was no denying that he was mine. It made shit worse when my mother met him and fell in love. What I realized was, even if she was just a side chick, she was also the mother of my son.

The second thing I didn't like about her just happened recently. In the past Clever was always been laid back and chill. Now if I wasn't on the phone with her everyday or at her crib every night she would send hateful messages.

I didn't want two wives.

If Clever didn't shape up I was going to cut her off and find another cutie to fill her place. She was replaceable. My wife wasn't.

By Shay Hunter

When my phone vibrated in my pocket again my face went from compassion to anger toward Rain. Instead of holding her lovingly I pushed her back and paced the room. "You know what, I'm sick of this shit." I yelled at her. "Fuck you want me to do, Rain? Not get out on these streets and make money?" I paused. "Huh? You know how much this condo costs a month? Huh? $2,500! If I don't make paper you don't get to go to college or have this life." I paused. "If you don't understand that maybe I should bring somebody in here who does."

Her eyes widened and she shook her head no. She rushed up to me and said, "Baby, I didn't mean it like —"

"How you mean it then?" I walked away from her and plopped down on the edge of the bed. "Every night you nagging and acting like a kid. You got a nigga not wanting to come home at all."

She walked slowly toward me and I could tell she was trying to calm down. I felt bad for her but I needed to go through these lengths just to get out the house. I had two situations brewing at the same time. The one here with my wife and the one in Baltimore with my side chick.

"I don't mean to be fussy, Devin. I just love spending time with you." She sat next to me. "Am I wrong for that? We been together for five years. And we used to have so much fun together. Why did that change?"

"Because of this shit right here. Either you gonna stop coming at me 'bout stupid shit or we through." I leaped up and headed toward the bedroom door. "I thought you were stronger than this, Rain. Maybe I chose wrong." I grabbed my wallet and keys off the table by the door and stormed out.

By Shay Hunter

CHAPTER THREE

RAIN

When my husband left I dropped to my knees and cried my eyes out until I couldn't cry anymore. I loved him so much and the last thing I wanted him to think was that I didn't trust him. It's just that there are so many ratchet hoes out here that would kill to be in my shoes. I see them when we go out. I hear their little comments about how sexy he is and how much they would love to lick his chocolate head. Devin loved the comments but I didn't find them funny. I felt disrespected and although I didn't want him fighting no female, I wanted him to stick up for me. He knew I wasn't the fighting type. My mother and father are evangelists and that kind of stuff didn't go on in my house.

Sometimes I appreciated that my husband was so hot but other times I resented his looks. It didn't help that he drove a big sexy black Range Rover, or that he was tall and had money in his pocket. He's the kind of nigga that when you saw him you wanted him all to yourself. That's why I hated when he left the house. The entire time Devin and I had been married I never found any indications that he was cheating.

But why was I so sure that he was?

Picking myself up off the floor I moped to the couch lifted my home phone and called my best friend. It rang once before she answered. "What's up girl? You coming over here tonight?"

"Jonie, I need you to do me a favor," I sighed.

"Speak on it, bitch."

"Devin is about to pull out of the parking lot." I sniffled. "Can you come down here real quick and follow him for me again?"

By Shay Hunter

"How you know he not gone already? You know he drives like a bat out of hell."

"Not sure how a bat out of hell drives but I know he's here. I can still see the headlights shining on the living room window. Plus you know he never pulls off right away. He gotta smoke a cigarette; find the right song and all that other crazy shit. But hurry up before he leaves."

"Are you okay, Rain?" she asked in a compassionate tone. "Cause you sound bad."

"I won't be okay if I lose my husband."

CHAPTER FOUR
CLEVER

When he said he was coming to the club to get his bitch, me of course, I didn't believe him. Devin had a history of telling me he was on his way and never showing up. But sure as he was sexy, I was sitting in VIP with another nigga's arm wrapped around me like I belonged to him. You would've thought I had the wedding ring instead of his wife.

He stomped up to me, grabbed me by my elbow and snatched me away from Lotus' embrace. I thought it was the sexiest thing he'd ever done and a smile spread on my cheeks as I was being snatched through the club like a bag of trash.

By Shay Hunter

We argued for a few minutes and before I knew it I was sitting in the back of his truck riding his dick with my arms wrapped around his neck. His hands were on both sides of my waist as he talked that good shit in my ear. "You thought you was gonna give my pussy away? Huh? Did you think I was gonna let that bamma ass nigga in there fuck you?"

"No, baby," I moaned as a tear rolled down my left cheek. I felt like I was riding a wild bull as he pumped in and out of me.

"Fuck you doing up under another nigga then?" he pushed into me hard forcing a sharp pain to roll in my lower abdomen. "You trying to get that nigga killed? Huh?"

"No, baby," I whimpered. "You know I wouldn't do you like that. I just thought you didn't want me no more," I continued as I tightened my walls squeezing his dick in the process. "You gotta show me, Devin." I bucked my hips wider. "You gotta show me how you feel about me."

He gripped a wad of my hair in the back of my scalp and yanked so hard that my neck was exposed. Slowly he ran his warm tongue from the bottom of my throat to the top of my chin causing chills all over my body. "I'm not trying to hear that shit you talking, bitch," he said as I could feel his stick pulsating. "If I ever catch another nigga in my playground I'll kill you." He stroked me harder. "You hear me!"

I was too busy feeling good to respond. As he continued to work his magic I gripped his shoulders and bore down onto him as hard as I could. I wanted his entire dick inside of me. "I'm cumming, D. Please don't stop."

"Fuck I want to stop for?" he asked. "Huh? When the pussy feel this good." He said one more thing I couldn't make out before he splashed his semen into my body.

As much as I was feeling Devin I didn't understand why he couldn't pull out when he came. Whenever I brought up the idea of him wearing a condom he'd say some dumb shit like, 'If I want to wear a condom I'll just fuck a pillow instead. I'd probably feel the same thing. Nothing.'

I tried to take birth control but I was always so lazy with the days that it didn't work. I think I was going to get the birth control shit in my arm and be done with it for good. Pulling out when he was cumming was only one of the things he didn't like. He also didn't like me to shave my hair too close on my pussy or wash up after I came from the gym so he could smell me. He had a lot of requests for a nigga who didn't belong to me.

He was stroking my back and looking into my eyes. "Damn that shit felt so —"

His sentence stopped shortly and he looked over my shoulders with gaping eyes. Thinking a stick up boy caught us slipping I turned around only to see a girl standing in front of the car with her arms crossed over her chest.

"Get up for a sec, Clever," he said pushing me off of him. He tucked his dick down, pulled up his boxers and zipped up his jeans. With his belt hanging open he got out of the truck and approached her.

I sat down, and repositioned my clothes as I tried to hear what he was saying. Who was this chick? Another side bitch?

"Fuck you doing here, Jonie?" he asked with a frown on his face as he adjusted his belt. "Snooping?"

"You don't get to ask questions, Devin," she responded with her hand flipped palm up. "Now stop bullshitting. It's time for you to cash me out. I let you cum when I could've rolled up on you earlier and knocked your grove. Now you know the routine. Where it at?"

Devin shook his head, reached inside his pocket and pulled out a few bills. It was hard to see exactly how much but I saw at least three Benjamin's. "You a no good ass bitch," he said slapping them in her palm. "I hope a truck fall on your fucking head and you die."

She didn't seem bothered in the least at how he was going on her. Instead she rolled her eyes and counted the money in front of him. "Miss me with all of that shit. You the one doing my friend wrong by sleeping with your whore in the back of a club." She shook her head. "Why you doing broke nigga shit with that bitch when you got money?"

Hearing her call me out of my name I lifted the latch to get out of his truck, opened the door and plopped out. I wanted to hear her say that shit to my face. This chick didn't know anything about me and if I was a whore Devin was the same as far as I was concerned.

Devin must've heard the door open because he turned around and with a lowered brow yelled, "Get back in the fucking ride!" When I continued to approach he said, "Don't make me fuck you up, Clever! Get back inside!"

"Let me find out this cunt's name is Clever," she giggled. "It's creative if nothing else. I'll give her that."

Not trying to start a fight with him I walked back to the door. But not without saying, "Since you know my name remember it, slut. Don't call me out my name again. You might get more than your feelings hurt."

She tried to move toward me until Devin pushed her so hard she stumbled backwards and fell on her ass. Instead of helping her up he said, "You got your money, Jonie! Bounce!"

She stood up, brushed her ass off and looked at me and then Devin. "You know the foulest shit of all?"

"What's that?" he snapped.

"That before now I thought you were just fucking that slut. Now I know the truth. You fell in love with her."

Instead of stomping her out for calling me out of my name again I grinned. Besides, her words were like music to my ears.

CHAPTER FIVE

RAIN

As I looked at my best friend Jonie and my cousin Nikki who were standing in the middle of my living room I was slightly relieved. Still something felt off. She claimed he wasn't cheating but why was my woman's intuition firing off?

"Are you sure you didn't see another girl?" I asked scratching my short curly brown hair. "Because something didn't feel right. When Devin left earlier I got the impression that he was going to see somebody else."

My cousin Nikki walked around me toward my kitchen and Jonie and me followed her. "I don't get it. If Jonie said he wasn't cheating why push the issue?" She opened the fridge and grabbed one of Devin's beers, which I told her not to do. She sat her beefy frame in my black kitchen chair and popped the cap. "You act like you want him to be cheating or something." She gulped the beer.

"Yeah, Rain, I'm your best friend. If I thought the nigga was cheating do you think for one moment that I would let him get away with it? Come on now. You know me better than that." She leaned up against the refrigerator.

"So why was he acting so funny?" I asked to myself even though it came out my mouth aloud.

"You want my opinion?" Jonie asked.

"Yeah."

"I think you got a good husband who may be working harder to put you through school and to pay for this fly crib. You live in Georgetown and I don't have to tell you that shit ain't cheap. Try not to blow stuff out of proportion, Rain. You might lose your nigga."

Irritated with it all I plopped down in the seat across from my cousin and threw my face into my hands. If what she was saying was true I had to get myself together. I hear about chicks all the time losing their husbands due to accusing them of things they didn't do. I loved Devin and I wanted him to know that I could trust him.

Even though I couldn't.

As they talked amongst themselves I took a moment to think about when he asked me to marry him. We hadn't been speaking in three days because I was tired of feeling neglected. Ever since he made a decision, without asking me, that I couldn't hang out with him and go to school at the same time he was never home. And when I asked him to chill with me he never had time and then suddenly, one day, that changed.

"Get dressed," he said as he walked inside the house. "I'm gonna take you to the movies."

He went from giving me no attention to taking me out. Just like that I was watching a movie with Denzel Washington that I begged him to see weeks earlier. I didn't know what got into him but in the middle of the movie, during one of the best scenes, he moved around in his seat a little before looking directly at me.

It was dark but I could still see the whites of his eyes. My heart thumped because I just knew he was about to break up with me. "I know this is not the right time but I told myself I would ask you the moment I got up the nerve," he whispered. "I knew I had to do it no matter where we were or I might punk out." He wiped the sweat off his forehead with a napkin drenched in popcorn butter. "Rain, will you be my wife?"

I didn't answer him right away. I thought it was a joke until I saw the glow from the movie screen bounce off the ring in his hand. I was so excited that I threw my arms around him and screamed yes. A few people yelled at us because we were making noise and Devin said a few words to them before we walked out.

That was the happiest day of my life. But it wasn't until after we were married, at the Justice of the Peace, that I figured there was something else driving the proposal. Something that made him so guilty that he wanted me to marry him before I found out. I thought it might be another woman or that he got somebody pregnant but I never found out. For the earlier part of my marriage I waited for some female to come out of nowhere and tell me that my husband was hers. But as the years went by nothing happened and I told myself

By Shay Hunter

I was looking too much into things. But now...well now I'm not so sure.

Needing to do some more investigation myself I got up from the table and walked toward my bedroom. "Where you going?" Jonie asked.

"I gotta check on something right quick. I'll be back." I walked in my bedroom and closed the door. I didn't feel like answering questions. I needed to know if Devin was cheating on me and why I felt so strongly about it.

When the door was closed I heard Jonie whisper to my cousin. "She always making shit out to be more than what it is. Most bitches would be happy they nigga not cheating. Damn!"

"Girl, you know how dry my cousin is sometimes. All she gonna do is go in there, cry and be up Devin's ass again."

They could talk shit all they wanted. They didn't have a husband and until they got one they couldn't tell me what to do with mine. I sat on the edge of my bed, grabbed my red Mac book and logged onto the Internet.

Two months ago I put a feature on Devin's phone where I could track his whereabouts. A few days after I added the feature he was home more and started to do things with me so I took it off and promised myself I would never add it again. I figured I could trust him and there was no need to follow him.

I guess I was wrong.

CHAPTER SIX

CLEVER

I had cheddar eggs in the frying pan on the stove, bacon in the oven and a pitcher of Mimosa on the kitchen table and it was all for my baby. I don't know what made Devin come over early in the morning but I'm glad he did. When I asked him what made him see me again since we already fucked in his truck the night before, he said something about his wife acting funny and he didn't feel like dealing with her.

Shit, I was cool with it if he was. Since he had the keys I was pleasantly surprised when he woke me up with some stiff dick. I played with my pussy the night before, replaying our session in his truck, so when he slid inside of me this morning I was wet and tight. It was sweet but this is the kind of thing that messes me up about Devin. He doesn't mind reminding me that I'm not the wife and should stay in my place but then when he does shit like this I get confused.

When the food was done I grabbed a red plate for Devin and a small yellow plastic bowl for Village so that I could put his baby food inside of it. I asked my aunt, who stayed in my son's room last night; if she wanted anything to eat but she mumbled something I couldn't hear in her usual attitude. It was no surprise that she didn't like Devin but I told her time after time it wasn't her place to talk to me about him. I didn't bother her and the many men she had paying her bills, rent or car note. So why was she always in my situation? Devin may be married but he kept money in my pockets and when her dudes failed to payout she didn't mind asking me for a few bucks.

By Shay Hunter

After the plates were on the table I scooped up Devin's food and he smacked me on my ass and licked his lips as he looked at it as if he'd never seen it before. "Why the fuck are you so sexy, Clever?"

I giggled knowing he was a sucker for the black stretch pants I wore. When I didn't wear panties, like now, you could see the imprint of my pussy and ass. "Because I want you to have a reason to come back. Why? Is it working?"

He grabbed his fork and scooped his eggs. "Don't play with me, sexy. You already know what it is." He stuffed his mouth.

With Devin taken care of I focused on the hallway and yelled, "Auntie, can you bring Village out so I can feed him?"

Devin shook his head when I said her name. I guess he knew she was about to talk shit because she didn't hide how she felt about him. Sure enough she came sliding into the hallway with Village on her hip. Her jet-black hair was pulled tightly in a ponytail exposing her pretty face. My aunt was in her forties but she could pass for late twenties easily. Her body was as tight as mine but when it came to the game of life she always talked like she was one hundred years old. Thought she knew everything and I never bought her shit.

The moment my aunt saw Devin she rolled her eyes. "Why is your shiftless ass not home with your wife? I know she looking for you."

Devin chewed what was in his mouth, sat his fork down and said, "Bitch, just give me my son and worry 'bout why you can't get dick if you paid a nigga."

She stomped over to Devin and stuffed my baby in his arms harder than I wanted. I was going to check her for tossing my child but he wasn't crying and I didn't feel like arguing with my aunt. Besides, when they beefed I stayed out of the way because I always seemed to make shit worse. For instance the last time I got involved in an argument between them we were in the grocery store. Rain was out of town and Devin decided to kick it with me for the week. They argued over the pettiest shit the entire time he stayed with me. My aunt felt the baby should eat Gerber food while Devin felt I should make his food for him fresh because he didn't like the ingredients. In the end I bought fresh fruit and bottles of baby food just to shut them up. After the fight was over, they didn't talk to me for three weeks, thinking I was taking sides.

"How would you know what I'm getting, nigga?" my aunt asked. "You fucking too many bitches to keep up with me or the dick I'm enjoying. Today you fucking my niece, tomorrow you'll be fucking your wife. Do yourself a favor and keep your own scoreboard."

"Auntie, please don't!" I yelled as I walked her over a plate.

"I'm not eating nowhere this no account nigga at," she said waving me off. "And you shouldn't either." She grabbed a glass out of the counter and poured some Mimosa inside of it. "Anyway I'm waiting on my ride to take me to get my hair done. Since you wouldn't let me use your car while mine is in the shop."

Devin laughed as he fed Village and wiped the corners of his mouth with a paper towel. I loved the fact that Village was his only child and it happened to be a boy. To me there was nothing cuter than seeing them together. "Fuck you wanna drive a car I bought her for?" Devin asked. "Don't forget what you just said. You don't like me remember?"

She rolled her eyes at him.

By Shay Hunter

"I couldn't let you use the car because I have to take Village to get a check up, Auntie," I interrupted. "Otherwise it wouldn't be a problem. You know that."

She rolled her eyes at Devin again and looked at me. "It's okay, Clever. I made arrangements anyway." She paused. "But I will tell you this, one day this nigga gonna have to make a choice and when he does it won't be you."

When there was a knock at the door she walked over to it and opened it without looking out of the peephole. I felt gut punched when I saw who was on the other side. Since my aunt's head was turned in my direction she didn't see who was at the door but I did. She must've seen the horror in my eyes because when she spun around she saw what had me shook.

It was Rain and two other girls, including the one I saw last night. I knew what his wife looked like because when she called and I was with him her face

Hoetic Justice 65

showed up on his cell phone. The other bitch I never saw a day in my life but what were they doing at my house?

"Who the fuck are you?" My aunt asked them.

"Bitch, my husband is in this house!" Rain yelled.

My aunt tried to slam the door in her face but it was too late. The three of them bullied their way into my apartment, yelling and screaming the entire time. My baby was crying at the top of his lungs and this didn't do anything but send me over the edge. Rain was violating big time with this shit. Since I been fucking Devin I never once popped up over his house and disrespected her place like she's doing now.

The moment he saw them Devin stood up and I rushed to get the baby. With my child safely out of his arms I rushed Village to his crib, slammed the door and headed back toward the scuffle. I don't know who this bitch thinks she is but she got me fucked up. And

By Shay Hunter

she was going to know me too. "What you doing in my house you bum bitch?" I yelled stepping up to Rain.

Instead of approaching me she walked around me like I was a ghost and approached Devin. But I pushed her sending her face first into the sofa. After that you could say things got out of control. My aunt stole the girl from last night and I got to rumble the fatter chick. One on one the girl wasn't no match for me and I was punishing her pudgy ass. Through the fist throws and the wild arms I could see Devin and Rain yelling at each other but too much was going on for me to make out what was being said. The only thing I was thinking was that I hoped this wasn't it between Devin and me. I hoped he wouldn't be able to not see me again due to getting caught. The mere thought made me punish the girl I was wrecking even more.

The fight seemed to move back and forth and before long the kitchen table was lying sideways on the floor and the pitcher of Mimosa was spilled over the eggs and Village's baby food.

Through it all somehow I was able to get on top of the chick I was wrecking. She was on the floor; face up trying to get a blow. She would've had a better chance fighting somebody in another country she was so bad.

Tiring of her I lowered my head and bit her face. I was about to bite her again when she pushed me off with the strength of forty men and ran out the front door. Leaving her people behind.

When I looked to my left my aunt was handling her own with Jonie and didn't need my help. Auntie had that chick up against the wall as she landed blow after blow on her face. Blood was all over the walls and my apartment looked like a horror scene.

With my hands free, since the other girl ran, I yanked Rain by the back of the hair as she continued to yell at Devin. It was now time for me to deliver her the same fate as I did her friend. I was about to scratch her eye sockets out when Devin pushed me back so hard the back of my head slammed into the front doorknob. With me out the way he went back to fussing at his wife.

When I looked at my auntie I could tell she was about to leave the chick when she saw what he did but I put my hand up telling her I was okay. She went back to business and I was relieved because I needed to digest what just happened. Although things were moving fast I needed the time to take in what was going on. Did he just choose her over me? I know he's married to her but up until this point I always thought I had a place in his life. Didn't I deserve a little more respect?

Sitting on the floor I rubbed the back of my head trying to relieve some of the throbbing pain and looked up at him in a confused manner. "Why did you do that?" I yelled while he was talking to Rain.

"Because I wasn't about to let you touch my wife, bitch," he yelled as if he didn't even know me.

Upon hearing his words my heart throbbed and I could feel tears welling up in my eyes. The same nigga with keys to my house, who was just inside of my body hours earlier, was treating me as if I didn't matter.

Instead of realizing she won Rain yelled, "Oh, now I'm your fucking wife!" she paused wiping tears from her face. "Because it don't look like it! What the fuck are you doing here, Devin? Help me understand!"

I never knew pain like this. Not even when I was with Ranch. It was different between Devin and me. Unlike with Ranch I knew my place. I allowed Devin to have his wife and my body too. I played the games and never disrespected or threatened to call his wife and still he treated me like shit.

"You know you my wife," he said to her softly. "I was just in here waiting on my man Crisp. That's his bitch, baby." He pointed at me like I was some old portrait he forgot to take off the wall. "Come on, Rain. You know me better than that. I would never disrespect you. You know I like my women classy. I mean look at that slut. Look at the nasty ass pants she's wearing. She could never be with me. She ain't my type!"

Although he was disrespecting me I didn't have the energy to fight back. Instead I took the verbal beat down he dished like he was right. I was weak emotionally and physically.

"Was that your baby?" Rain asked sobbing. "The one that was sitting on your lap when I busted up in here?" she paused. "Just be honest, Devin!"

Hoetic Justice 71

"Fuck no that's not my kid!" he hollered. "Are you crazy?"

And that's when the little spirit I had left disappeared. He denied his son and me in the same day. My shoulders hunched over and my head drooped lower. So many tears covered my eyes that I couldn't see him anymore. He was as blurry as the relationship I thought we had.

When he calmed her down he put his arm around her shoulder like an invisible robe and yelled at the girl my auntie was whipping. "Come on, Nikki. We gotta bounce."

Beaten and out of breath, Nikki pulled herself up off the floor.

While they walked toward the door I waited for him to look down at me. To give me one sign that I was more important to him than he was letting off. But when his eyes met mine he glared at me as if he never wanted to see me again. And I knew immediately I had my answer.

It was over.

It had been a week since I'd seen my man and I was fucked up mentally.

I could hear Village crying in his room but I couldn't get out of bed to go see about him. I didn't feel like doing anything. Not talking to anybody, not eating and not feeding my baby.

Over the past few days I finally realized something I never wanted to admit. I was past being in love with him. I was pressed and had no self-respect. He could treat me any way he wanted just as long as he was in my life.

Realizing two hours passed since I called him today I picked up the phone. I almost fell out of the bed when he answered. "Devin, it's me. Clever." For some reason I lost my swag and couldn't get what I wanted off my heart. "What you doing? I mean, why haven't you called?"

"What you want, Clever?" he asked. His tone was cold and full of no nonsense.

"I know she probably getting on your nerves over there," I said trying to make her look bad as usual. "If you want I can call her and tell her I'm Crisp's girlfriend like you said. And we can meet somewhere else since she knows where I live now."

"Listen, bitch, leave me the fuck alone! I'm here with my wife!"

He slammed the phone down and I was gut punched yet again. I swore to myself that I would never fall for another after my fiancé and I did it

By Shay Hunter

anyway. I hated feeling the way that I did and I didn't know what to do with my emotions. Before this shit I had a solid motto that I lived by. It was simple and to the point.

Fuck niggas! Get money!

But here I was looking crazy. I missed Devin so much it ripped at my insides. I had no clue how to start over. Who would be my sugar daddy now? When I heard my front door open I popped up in bed with a sudden burst of energy.

Devin was here!

Maybe Devin couldn't talk a moment ago and had to be cold because she was around him.

Now he was at my house and I hadn't washed my pussy in days.

Plus I looked a fucking mess. If he saw me like this he would be glad he left me and chose his wife. I had to get up and wash my body. I dipped into the bathroom, slammed the door and happily yelled, "I'll be right out, baby." I turned the water on and did a whore's bath, which consisted of running the water, smearing soap on my rag and wiping my hot parts.

Since he was back the plan was to feed Village, cook Devin a hot breakfast and drop to my knees to suck the skin off his dick. It would be my way of apologizing even though I didn't know what I did wrong. Once I was clean I slid on my purple silk robe and pulled the bathroom door open. My heart dropped in my gut when I saw my auntie, Vanessa and Tracy standing on the other side.

"Judging by the look on your face I take it you're not happy to see us," my auntie said. "Too, bad. You should've answered the phone."

By Shay Hunter

"I don't know why you mad at us," my aunt said as she sat on the recliner across from Village and me in the living room. "If you would've answered the phone we wouldn't be here." She stood up and took Village out of my arms. Then she grabbed his food. "I mean lets be serious, Clever. You let the nigga run you into the dirt. What's wrong with you?"

As she held Village in her arms and fed him I saw how his eyes widened and a smile spread across his face as he looked at me. Even though I was less than a mother over the past few days I could tell he still loved me. The guilt moved over my body like a cold blanket and I made myself a silent promise. Love or hate, I would never make my baby go through the pain I was feeling again. No matter what Devin and me did behind closed doors Village didn't deserve to be exposed to it. Whether we got back together or not, from here on out I would live for my baby until my dying day.

"I didn't feel like talking to anybody," I said to my aunt as I pulled my knees to my chest. "Anyway I'm an adult and am entitled to my feelings. If I don't want to be bothered I don't want to be bothered."

"I hear what you saying but I still can't believe you fell in love with that nigga," Vanessa said. I didn't feel like her talking down to me and I was liable to say something she didn't like. "You knew he wasn't yours. You knew he was on loan."

"Vanessa, will you please stop acting holier than thou because you not," Tracy said. "If Clever didn't get with that nigga some other chick would have."

"Why do you keep talking to this girl like giving a man your body without commitment is okay?" Vanessa asked as she sat on the couch and thumbed through her social network page. "If a man is not willing to commit you shouldn't give him your heart. Whether she has sex or not with him she was wrong for going too deep emotionally." She looked at Village. "Don't get me wrong, Vill is an adorable baby but Clever crossed the line a long time ago."

"Don't talk about my baby," I snapped. "And you talk all that shit but your nigga has yet to welcome the sunrise with you either," I reminded her as Devin's face flashed through my mind and I struggled to push it out. "If I'm a side chick you are too."

"It's not about being a side chick. It's about expecting better when the situation is less," Vanessa responded. "He is not your man. Never was. Do you really think Devin would be serious about you even if Rain wasn't in the picture?"

"Yes," I said although I wasn't sure.

"The answer is no," Vanessa said as if she were correcting me. "I mean why should a man wife you?

Why should a man want to be with you for the long run? Why should he love you when you don't love yourself." She tossed her phone in her purse. "Niggas like Devin will only treat you as good as you treat yourself. Nothing more and nothing less. Women need a man but only if he belongs to her."

"So you think being single is wrong?" Tracy asked with a frown on her face.

"It ain't about being single."

"Well you sound like you saying a bitch can't live without having a man." Tracy walked toward the fridge, grabbed one of Devin's beers and sat on the other end of the couch. "Let me tell you something and hear me good. Pussy runs the world."

Vanessa frowned like what Tracy said stunk. "How you sound?" she leaned in. "I mean do you actually believe what you're saying or do you just talk for points?"

"Bitch, I'm dropping knowledge. Consider any country in any part of the planet and bet money that a woman was behind the formation. A man can't do shit without a cold bitch so for real we don't need them." She snapped her fingers. "Believe that."

While my friends talked my head off I was surprised that my auntie was so quiet. She was a highly opinionated woman and sometimes her views got in the way of what I wanted to do in life. Most times her answer for my troubles consisted of me leaving Devin, asking for more money I didn't need, or meeting new niggas. But now she was silent and for some reason it made me uncomfortable. When Village's eyes closed she walked him to his room and came back empty-handed. "Both of ya'll are confused," my auntie said.

Vanessa and Tracy frowned.

"How you figure?" Vanessa asked.

"You don't need a man and yet he is crucial to the survival of a woman."

Vanessa laughed. "Do tell."

"Obviously none of us would be in existence without a man's nut and yet a woman is required to carry a child to full term. With all that said to say a man is not essential is ridiculous. A relationship might not be necessary but both a man and woman are necessary for survival." She paused. "So the goal is always to conquer. To be the dominant sex."

I sat up straight suddenly interested in what my auntie had to say. She was militant when it came to men but I felt like I needed her cold words right now. Devin was doing him, probably proposing to his wife again or some shit, and I was sitting here with a dry pussy and a broken heart. Maybe auntie had it right all along and now it was time for me to realize it.

"What you talking about, Annette?" Tracy asked.

"As women we should always be thinking what could we do to conquer a man. Through conquering we build strength. We can take care of our families, our children and hold shit down when men fall weak. But in order to do that you must first learn the level of your power because all women are not created equally. On a scale from one to ten some women may rank a six in strength while others may reach as high as ten."

Obviously interested Tracy said, "Describe someone who would be on the lower end."

"Well someone who ranks a one may have the power to suffer through all of her man's indecencies but have nothing to take care of herself. She's basically a doormat and I don't respect these kinds of women. Her hair and her body will probably suffer and she's more than likely a big woman who can cook, please her man sexually and act as if he's doing nothing wrong even though he cheats in her face. While a woman with the power ranking of a ten can cook, fuck, take care of the family and have the power to bring a man to his knees if he gets out of line. When she rejects his love he will not survive. If this woman is the wife she'll get a bigger ring but if she's the side chick the power she has over him will be even greater."

My friends busted out laughing but I was glued onto every word. My heart suddenly pounded. "How do you know if you are a ten?" I asked.

"You have to put yourself through 'The Test'. All women do."

"But how?"

"It won't be easy, Clever. Most women can't go a day without giving into their dude. In order to reach ten status you have to be able to cut him off even if you love him harder than any woman in his life. You have to be willing to give tough love and you must be relentless. Only then will you bring him to his knees."

"I want to be a ten."

"Then I'll help you get their, niece. It's time for some hoetic justice."

CHAPTER SEVEN
DEVIN

I been in this house for three weeks straight after Rain showed up over Clever's apartment and still my wife is crying. What she want me to do? I'm fucking home! Her weakness was getting on my nerves and I had no pity in my heart for her.

"Are you listening, Devin?" she sniffled.

"Why you keep asking me that?" I was sitting on the toilet and she was in the tub crying her eyes out.

"Because you seem like you're mind is somewhere else. I'm trying to talk to you. I'm trying to find out what I can do to make our marriage stronger."

I'm sick of this shit!

Don't get me wrong I love my wife. Contrary to what some people think niggas don't marry broads

By Shay Hunter

unless there's a need or desire. For me I married her because I really love her.

But I miss my shawty too.

When I first got with Cleverly I thought it was just about sex. But as the weeks rolled by and she fell back and stopped calling me, I realized I fell harder than planned because now I was worried. Was she fucking some other nigga? You gotta understand shawty is fun to be around. Unlike my wife she's a video gamer and when I want my dick sucked she never hits me with the, 'I did you now you gotta do me shit' some chicks throw.

She makes me feel like the shit and is always about me and for that she gets money and my time. I don't have to throw bills at broads just because I got it, 'cause every chick don't deserve to get a payday. But Clever is the mother of my child and I like kicking it with her.

I ain't gonna lie, when Clever told me she was pregnant with my kid I was worried. I thought she would find my wife and tell her about Village. But she stood strong. Even when we argued she never threatened to approach my wife or tell her about our relationship or my son. She understood her place and respected it. If I couldn't come over she was all, "No problem, baby. See me when you see me." Or if I made business plans across the state line and I couldn't see her for weeks at a time she would say, "I know you gotta work papi. We'll do us when you get back."

Add that along with the fact that she could fuck and there was no reason for me to cut her off. She even did a good job of birthing the cutest kid I could ask for. I felt bad that I couldn't introduce him to my moms who I was close with yet but I knew in time that would change. I was falling in love with the kid too much to deny him.

By Shay Hunter

Yeah, shit was good until Rain showed up at Clever's place with Jonie and Nikki. How the fuck did she find me? When I dropped her off home later that day I searched around my car, inside of it and even on the top and I didn't see a device. I don't know how she did it but I had plans to find out.

"You've been acting so fake lately, Devin. Do you miss her?" Rain asked me.

Yes I missed the fuck out of Clever. I can't say that I was in love but I could say that with the dope boy lifestyle I led Clever helped make shit okay. My wife was good. She kept a clean house, made sure my meals were cooked every night and gave me mind-blowing sex. But with all that said she was still boring. All she wanted to do was study to be a doctor. What about a niggas's needs when food or sex was not a requirement? I needed mental stimulation and if it wasn't for Clever I doubt I'd be married to her ass long.

"I told you I don't know that chick," I said.

She started sobbing loudly.

"Rain, why you crying?" I said trying to keep the anger out of my voice. "I been in the house early every night even though you know I have shit to do on the streets. Haven't I shown you that I love you?"

She sniffled and long lines of snot rolled over her lips. As usual. "I feel like you gonna leave me," she sobbed in between hiccups. "I know you were fucking that bitch, Devin! I know it!"

"That's what I'm trying to say...you wrong! Fuck I look like fucking that girl? She not even my type!"

"Yes she is," she said as she moved around in the tub a little. I think she farted too because I smelled something on the half. "She's dark skin, short and got a big ass just like you like! If anything she looks just like me!"

I sighed. "Bay, on my life that's my man's girl," I said raising one hand in the air while the other rested on my heart. "You even talked to him last night and he told you. It's like I'm doing everything in my power to let you know that I want to be your husband and still it's not enough." I paused. "You charging me with being with a bitch whose apartment we cut work in. That's fucked up, ma, because I would think you'd know me better than that."

"But what about that baby?"

"What about it?"

"He had your eyes!"

I stood up from the toilet and leaned on the sink. The annoying sensation I felt as I looked down at her drove me crazy. She had no idea how bad I wanted to say fuck it. How bad I wanted to roll out and never see her again. But she wasn't some bum bitch. She was my wife. Not only that, Rain did shit for me most responsible chicks would never do.

In the earlier part of our relationship she rented apartments in her name so I could hustle out of. She ran packs up and down the highway if I needed. She proved over and over she was down for me and I knew I needed to treat her better...but I hated when she was like this and I missed my Feel Good. I missed Clever.

"Rain, I told you before the kid wasn't mine. Just cause you see a baby in my lap don't mean I helped make it." I paused. "You know what. I'm gonna let you be by yourself for a little while. I've been here everyday over a week without going to work to help you get rid of this insecure shit and nothing works." I walked toward the bathroom door and I could hear her get out of the tub. But it was too late.

I was out the door.

Needing an emotional break I slid in my car and cruised down the block. I was doing all I could to not go over Clever's house because my wife knew the address. But my dick was pulsating just thinking about how she jacked and sucked my dick off at the same time.

Instead of using my keys to re-enter Clever's crib I shook my head and rode over my man's Prize and Mace's spot instead. They shared a condo in Washington DC that was nothing but a playboy palace. Bitches of different nationalities and intentions rolled in and out of their place everyday. And next to Clever's apartment it was the only other place that Rain didn't want me to go.

I knocked on the door and the moment I smelled vanilla incense and saw my man Prize's extra red Asian like eyes when he opened the door, I knew they had females in the spot. Mixed with black and Chinese Prize kept a fresh chick on his arm at all times because women loved looking at him. "Aw shit," he yelled into the condo when he saw me. "The boss is here!"

When he opened the door and I heard women scream I knew they were filled to capacity. "I'll come back," I told him. The last thing I needed at the time was some more female trouble. If my wife stopped by here and saw this shit it would be on.

"Nigga, get ya bitch ass in here," Prize said yanking me inside. "You here for a reason. Let's get to it."

Against my will I walked into their place. Every piece of white leather furniture was dressed with a different bitch. Light skin, dark skin, white and even a few exotics lay on the furniture wearing less than nothing. When I was fully inside a Brazilian looking beauty stood up the moment she saw me and moved toward my direction. But her trip was broken when Mace stepped into her path.

Although he was white he stayed tanned which confused some women who didn't know if he had a little black mixed in. Standing about 6'4 the Brazilian chick didn't stand a chance when he stepped in front of her and pushed her back. "Now I know it's about to be a party," he said bringing me into a manly embrace. "What you beefing with your wife or something?"

Irritated that he knew I wouldn't be over here under any other circumstance I said, "Fuck you talking 'bout? I go where I want."

Prize and Mace laughed. "Yeah, a'ight," Mace continued as he slapped one of the women's butts. Robotically the chick got up, grabbed a beer and handed it to me. "You know you wouldn't be over here unless you were having trouble in the palace. Now if it ain't the wife it's the mistress. Which one is it?"

Embarrassed I took a sip of the beer and said, "First off things are always sweet on my front. I'm just here to remind ya'll about the upcoming delivery. I don't have nobody I trust to make the drop so we need to discuss other options."

Since business was the topic Prize rubbed his eyes. He looked like he was trying to focus but it wasn't working. He was still fucked up. "You wanna step in the office and work it out?" he said.

I looked around the condo. Even if I was coming to talk business there were too many people. So I stopped faking it and said, "Naw, I'll get up with ya'll later."

"You sure?" Mace asked. "I got a bitch here that can suck your dick and fuck you at the same time?"

When he made the comment my dick jumped but I shook my head and regained focus after realizing that was impossible. Besides I wanted to see Clever and I was tired of waiting. "Nah, I'm good though. I'll get up with you later."

"No doubt," Prize said as I gave them both dap and walked out.

After all the procrastination and hesitation I finally ended up where I wanted to be the entire time...over Clever's. I was standing in front of her door with my fist balled up in a knot. I was just about to knock but decided I should call instead. Plus I wasn't trying to deal with her aunt if she was there.

So I took my cell phone out of my jean pocket and dialed her number. It rang once and then I heard it ringing inside of the apartment. Clever was there but why wasn't she answering the phone? I leaned my head against the door and pressed my ear against it. I knew she was standing right there so I knocked harder.

Instead of letting me in, I could hear footsteps walk away. It felt like a bowling ball rested in the pit of my stomach. I went from confused to angry. Was another nigga in there? Who was making her feel good? Moan or say his name?

I removed my key from my pocket and placed it in the doorknob. It was time to break the fucking apartment up if another nigga was inside. I was about to turn the knob and walk in until I remembered she wasn't mine.

It was over and I had to leave it alone.

Before leaving my head pressed against the door and I placed my hand on it as if I could feel her body again.

I let shit get complicated.

Fuck!

CHAPTER EIGHT
CLEVER

I sat on the edge of my bed while cupping my vagina through my panties. My pussy was throbbing like crazy. I was five seconds from rushing to the front door, snatching Devin inside and dropping to my knees. But my aunt was rubbing my shoulder saying, "You did the right thing. Stay strong."

Irritated with it all I stood up, walked away and looked down at her. "I don't know about this shit," I said as I paced the floor. "If I did the right thing why does it feel so bad?" I wanted a firm answer.

"Because you gave a nigga your heart without giving him the instructions. Just feel the burn, Clever. In the end you'll get your revenge and bring that nigga to his knees. Don't forget how he treated you. In your house. He deserves to be ignored."

I heard her but I wanted a better answer. One I could water and grow into the truth. Something that could help me understand why a woman should deny a man she loved even if they were not supposed to be together. "But he showed up! Why make him wait?"

"Because if you don't make him feel how bad it feels to not have you he'll never know he needs you." Her words rolled off smoothly. "Before he had the power and now you do."

I lowered my head and tried to rid myself of the throbbing sensation that was coursing through my clitoris. Since I felt weird to be so horny around my aunt I figured I'd go to the gym to relieve some stress. So I washed up, oiled my body and tossed on my gym clothes. Before leaving out I said, "I love him you know?"

"What are you saying? That you don't want my help? That you don't want revenge?"

"I'm not saying that. It's just that it hurts so bad."

"This is why not every bitch can get to the power level of ten. They care too much about the pain." She paused. "Let me bring him to his knees for you. And then you can decide what to do with him."

Another week passed and still I hadn't spoken to Devin. It still hurt but not as much. Maybe I was getting use to the separation. With a lot of shit on my mind I was lifting heavy on the squat machine. It felt good sweating because it always helps me relieve stress. My aunt was right. If Devin wanted to front like I wasn't a part of his life than he could be subtracted.

By Shay Hunter

I took a quick break and texted Tracy and Vanessa. I told them we were going out later on tonight so to get ready. They were excited when I said we would be going to the strip club and that VIP was on me. I couldn't believe I allowed myself to get so wrapped up into a man who didn't belong to me.

It was official.

I was done.

I was just about to do some chest presses on the bench when a fine ass dude walked up behind me. He stood over my head and touched the barbell softly. Looking down at me he said, "Can I spot you, ma?"

At first I was about to tell him of course. But he was too attractive and I decided to play hard to get from here on out. "I'm good." I gripped the bar and did my first push. "But thank you anyway."

He chuckled a little and said, "Now you know I'm not gonna be able to finish my workout if I leave right?"

I lifted twice more and said, "Why not?"

"Because the entire time I'm gonna be worried." He smoothed his hand down his waves and said, "That you gonna drop this weight on that pretty face." He winked. "Now come on, sexy. Let me spot you."

"Nah, slim," Devin said coming from what seemed like nowhere. "I got her."

Old boy's eyes widened and he looked at me once more, frowned and stepped away. Instead of Devin spotting me with the weights I already had he added ten more pounds. Lifting them over my head, he placed me in a position where I had to lift or die.

Struggling I pushed it up and said, "Devin, what you doing? Trying to kill me?"

"Don't ask me no questions. I should crack your fucking face. Now push this shit for you need reconstructive surgery."

I pushed the weight again and he lifted it up and sat it on the rack. When I tried to sit up he slammed me back down and said, "You not done your set." He gave me five seconds and handed me the bar again forcefully.

I pressed the barbell away from my face while trembling and sweating. I could feel the vein in the middle of my forehead pulsating. I knew my life was about to come to an end. In all of the years I'd been dealing with him he had never acted so possessive.

"Why...are...y-you mad at me?" I struggled to say.

"Because you playing games, bitch. I know you heard me knocking at your door last week. And I know you see my number on your cell. What you doing? Trying to carry me? While you riding around in the car

I bought you?" When he saw me shaking he took the weight from me. I tried to move but he said, "Stay down there. Where you belong." I saw his eyes whirling and I was scared even more for my life. "Now answer my question. Why you been ignoring me?"

Although he was threatening me with his eyes I hopped up anyway and looked up at him. Huffing and puffing I said, "You called me a whore, Devin! You pushed me on the floor in my own apartment. Fuck I look like being with you. You're done with me so let it be done!"

He waved me off. "I'm not trying to hear that shit! You know I didn't mean it like that. What you want me to do? Tell my wife I was cheating?" he paused. "Come on, Clever. You smarter than that!"

"No you wasn't supposed to tell her," I yelled. "I never asked you too either! But you cut me off. You wouldn't answer my calls and you hurt my feelings. You wouldn't even call to check on your son."

"But that didn't mean I didn't want to be with you!"

"How was I supposed to know? You consoled your wife in my apartment and left me on the floor. Like you weren't in my body earlier that day. Like I wasn't the mother of your son And didn't fuck you like a king before feeding you breakfast! You were out of pocket, Devin and I'm sick of the mental games."

He paced a little and I could see a few of the guys who were lifting suddenly looking at us. "Clever, you know I got a wife. If you with me then you gotta be with me even if it's time for war!"

I knew what he was saying was true. I was the side bitch. But then I heard my aunt's voice. This nigga wanted it all and he didn't care about me. You see shit would be different if we were just fucking without him telling me he loved me in my ear. Things would be different if he didn't cum in me and we didn't have a child. But he crossed the line before me so of course I would catch feelings.

The more shit he talked the angrier I got. It was time for me to bring this nigga too his knees. It was time to play the game. With a lowered head I said, "You're right, baby. It's just that I didn't know it would hurt so bad." He walked up to me and my pussy began to pulsate. But now shit was all business even if I did feel a little pleasure.

"I know it's fucked up, Clever, but you know I'm feeling you."

"But do you love me?" I asked. "Or were you saying what I wanted to hear all those times?"

I could tell he was searching his mind for an answer. "Why can't we be happy? Why can't we define what the rules are as we go along? Let's just do us and leave the terminology out of it?"

"Because I'm not going to let anybody else treat me as if I don't matter. I'm done with that." Remembering the script I said, "Sorry, D, but it's over." I grabbed my towel off the bench and moved toward the door. When I didn't feel him behind me I figured he was letting me walk out of his life. It would be better for him if he did.

But the moment I got next to my car I was yanked backwards and damn near dragged to his truck.

This nigga is whipped and I have him right where I wanted him.

I was standing inside my apartment, by the front door kissing Devin. We kissed so long that my bottom lip throbbed due to him sucking on it so hard. Although it felt good I was on some other shit.

Revenge.

Devin separated his lips from mine and looked down at me. For a second he gazed into my eyes. "I know I didn't say it but let me say it now. I'm sorry 'bout that shit that happened in here. Had I known Rain would've came at you like that I would've checked her 'long time ago." He kissed me on the lips. "You asked me something earlier in the gym."

"What was that?"

"Do I love you?"

"So what's the answer?" I grinned.

"It's yes," he kissed me again. "Now let me get out of here. I got money to make."

I opened the door and smiled but it felt plastic and I'm sure it looked just as fake to him. "Just call me when you can. Maybe we can play Madden tomorrow."

"Tomorrow?" he repeated. "I'm coming back here tonight." He kissed me again and left.

I locked the door and turned around only to see my aunt's face. "Don't you think you smiling a little too hard?" My aunt said as she walked out of the hallway with my baby on her hip. "I feel like we wasted time creating the plan if you not going to stick to it."

I walked over to her, took Village from her arms and sat on the couch with him. "If I don't do anything else I will be getting his ass back for how he treated me." I looked at my son. "How he treated us." I paused. "All you need to do is stand watch because it's going down."

CHAPTER NINE
RAIN

Tamar Braxton's CD was playing through the built in speakers inside of the wall and I was singing along with the lyrics to the song *Hot Sugar*.

♪ *I'll be his sweet little mama all the time.* ♪

♪ *And we can do it now or later that's fine.* ♪

♪ *He want that sugar...* ♪

♪ *He want that sugar...* ♪

Dancing in the kitchen I was making sure everything was perfect for dinner tonight. The biscuits were in the oven, the roast beef was sitting on top of the stove and I had Devin's favorite beer stocked up in the fridge. Earlier today I put his favorite glass mug in the freezer so it would be ice cold.

All I wanted to do was chill with my husband and talk about us. We had been together for a while and I

By Shay Hunter

was thinking about us having a baby too. Missing him, when I looked over at my cell phone, which was sitting on the counter, I was mad when I saw I missed his call. He tried to reach me three times by phone and sent four text messages but I was so busy cooking that I didn't see it.

I wiped my hand on the pink towel on the counter, grabbed my phone and called him back instead of reading the messages. The first time the phone rang four times with no answer. The second time I called it rang once and went straight to voicemail. Suddenly I had the uneasy feeling in my stomach that always preceded the worst times. He was on his shit again.

I just knew it.

Frustrated I ended the call and went through the text messages he sent.

First message: *Bay, give me a call.*

Second message: *Tryin' to reach you.*

Third: *Hit me on text. I don't have reception where I'm going.*

Fourth: *I won't be home til 2:00 am. Don't wait up.*

My stomach whirled and I tossed the phone on the floor, shattering the screen. I knew he was with that bitch. Why else wouldn't he answer the phone? I don't care what he says about her being Crisp's girl. Crisp was a fourteen-year-old kid who could never afford a girl who looked like her. That was his bitch and that probably was his kid too.

I'm getting real tired of Devin's shit.

I turned Tamar's CD off and played K. Michelle's song, *Can't Raise a Man.*

I was on my second bottle of wine and Jonie and Nikki were just as wasted, as I was two hours after I last tried to reach my husband. When I read the text that Devin wasn't coming home until late I decided to pass time with them. If I had some decent clothes in the closet I may have hit a club, something I hadn't done in years. But school and studying stole any hopes I had of a good wardrobe. Everything I owned was either a sweatshirt, t-shirt jeans or sweatpants. I was a homebody and now that I think about it, it was no wonder why he wanted another woman.

My hair was pulled back in a ponytail, as it always was. A heavy blue sweatshirt covered my upper body and grey sweatpants wiped away my lower body. Nothing about me was fuckable.

"Why do you keep saying the same shit?" Jonie asked me as she sat on the floor with her back against the couch. The place where Clever bit her cheek was stitched up and didn't look as bad as it first did. "You and me both know you not leaving Devin's ass."

"You don't know what I would do."

"Why would you even want to?" Nikki added. The two black eyes that older lady gave her were now green and trying to vanish. "I'll be damned if I give up my husband for a chick he not with." She shook her head. "You talked to Crisp and everything. He said she was his girl."

"Yeah, didn't you say that the girl called your cell phone the other day and left a message confirming that shit?" Jonie asked. "Just leave it alone, Rain. I hate to see you like this."

As they drilled me I picked up my cell phone like I had done so many times today. I was hoping to receive a text from him that said, 'I'm on my way' or 'I love you'. But he didn't contact me since the text messages and when I called he wasn't answering his phone.

Instead of getting relief from my friends that he probably wasn't cheating, I re-read the text messages a million times trying to find the underlining meaning. And now my battery was dead. With one percent battery left I tossed it on the couch and pouted.

"I don't know what I'm going to do right now but I do know I'm tired of being neglected. He's acting like its cool to spend so much time away from home. We might not have kids but he's married and I need him."

"You sound so stupid," Nikki said as she got up and sliced another piece of roast off as she stuffed it in her jaws. With her mouth full she said, "I'm tired of hearing about it too. If you think he's cheating either accept it or do something about and make a move. If not stop the complaining."

She was right. It was time for me to cuss that nigga out. I decided to send him a text but since my phone wasn't working I asked Jonie could I use hers. She slid it over to me and got up to grab a beer.

Since she had an Android and I had an Apple iPhone I never knew how to work hers. After a few taps I found myself in her picture file instead of the texting area. I flipped a few places trying to get to the home screen and my jaw dropped when I saw two pictures of Devin's truck. In one picture I saw the back of a girl with someone's hands on her lower back. But the second picture I saw the same girl but now Devin's face was looking over her shoulder. My heart thumped as I realized the chick was the same one in that apartment.

The one who supposedly belonged to Crisp.

Warm tears rolled down my face as I stood up and walked into the kitchen. Jonie and Nikki were talking about a picture that was circulating around of Chris Brown's large dick. But my face was tight and Jonie turned around and said, "Now what's wrong with you?" she joked. "A bitch answered his phone or something?"

Instead of answering I raised her phone showing the picture of my husband with another woman on his lap in the back of his truck. She snatched her cell from me and said, "Why you go through my shit? I thought you wanted to use the phone?"

I stepped further into the kitchen and yelled, "Why you fucking lie, Jonie? You told me you didn't catch him doing anything the night I had you following him!"

"I didn't!" she yelled.

"Then what are you doing with that picture?"

"Can you calm down first please?" she said stuffing her phone in her pocket.

"Bitch, don't tell me to calm down!" I stepped closer to her preparing to rock her head off but Nikki pulled me backwards by walking behind me and wrapping her arms around my body. "I could kill you."

"Fuck this shit," Jonie, said pushing past me. "If you don't want me over here I'm gone!" She walked to her purse and I shook Nikki off of me.

"I want you to tell me why you lied!" I yelled as I continued to approach her. "You my best friend!"

"Because I didn't want to hurt your feelings okay?" she yelled. "I wasn't trying to be the cause of your marriage not working. So I hid it from you. But now I wish I woulda just told you since it's obvious you gonna be with him regardless." She pulled the door open and stormed out.

By Shay Hunter

I can't believe after all of the pain he caused me that he was sleeping peacefully in his bed. Like everything was okay in his world. Meanwhile my entire existence was rocked. Everything I thought I had was a dream.

I stood in the bedroom doorway with a knife in my hand. I was spinning the sharp part on my index finger as I battled with stabbing him or letting him breathe. If he thought he was going to leave me without a fight he had another thing coming. He wouldn't get to post up in Baltimore and forget I ever existed.

Shit was about to get real.

When I accidently stabbed myself I tossed the knife on the floor and ran over toward him. What I need a weapon for when I could use my hands? "I hate you, mothafucka!" I screamed rushing over to him. "I fucking hate you for lying to me and I hope you die!"

He popped out of bed with wide eyes trying to defend himself. "Fuck is wrong with you?" he yelled covering his face as I scratched and slapped him everywhere my nails would land.

"I know, Devin! I know you fucked her!"

"What the fuck are you talking about?" he hollered as he managed to get me in a seated position on the bed. He sat behind me with his arms wrapped around my body preventing me from moving my arms to hit him again. I hated when he overpowered me especially when I was angry.

"I know you fucking that bitch! Jonie took a picture and I know! I saw her and you! Fucking in your truck! Why, Devin? Why break my heart like this?"

"What...pic...what...I...," he was stuttering and I knew immediately I was right. The funk of his morning breath made me angrier as I imagined it was because he ate that bitch's pussy the night before. "I'm sick of

By Shay Hunter

coming home to this bullshit!" he yelled suddenly.

"You gonna always believe another bitch before your own husband."

"If you got a problem with how I feel then don't come home no more!" I screamed. "I'm done!"

The moment I yelled those words he released the hold he had on me and I realized I messed up. I gave him the ammunition he needed to be with another woman and I couldn't take it back.

DEVIN

My wife went too far this morning. It's one thing to feel a certain way but it's a whole different story to put hands on me. Now if I would've busted her in the jaw she would've went crying home to her mother or called the police or some shit. I knew I couldn't trust Jonie's whore ass. I paid that bitch to be quiet and she showed her a picture of Clever and me anyway.

After that shit with my wife I needed a break but now was not the time. It was about 4:00 in the afternoon and I was about to get up with Crisp, Prize and Mace to discuss some business when my phone rang. It was Clever.

"What's up?" I said as I parked my truck in front of Prize and Mace's crib.

"What's up?" she repeated while yelling. "What's up is that bitch of yours came over my house and scratched up my fuckin car! That's what's up!"

Fuck!

The last thing I needed was this shit.

CHAPTER TEN
CLEVER

I was standing on the side of my car with my arms crossed over my chest while Devin examined the word BITCH scratched in my paintjob as if it were going to go away simply by staring. I thought it was hilarious that I framed his wife for doing this and then I started getting a lot of blocked calls on my cell phone. I knew it was that bitch. Now I feel totally justified in running a knife alongside my own car and blaming her. Besides, it was all part of the plan.

When Devin was done looking at the scratch as if it would go away he stood up and placed his hand over his face. "I can't believe she did this," he said before exhaling. "It's not like her."

That wasn't what I wanted to hear and his response almost sent me over the edge. I thought he would apologize, get me a new paint job and start looking at her differently. But here he was defending her again.

"So you saying I did this shit to my own car?" I asked placing my hands on my hips. Although I did he didn't know it.

"I'm not saying that," he said as he shook his head and stared at it again. "She just don't do stuff like this. Rain's a college girl. She be in the books. She don't be into no gangsta shit. Never has."

"Oh really?" I laughed sarcastically. "Is that the reason your face is scratched up right now? Because she's not into gangsta shit?" I paused. "Open your fucking eyes, Devin! Your wife's a psychopath. The last thing on her mind is respect for my property and if I were you I'd be careful. She might do something to you next."

"She wouldn't fuck with me," he said confidently. "She know better than to fuck with my shit."

"What if she does something worse?" I paused. "If I were you I'd really be careful, Devin. I'm just saying."

He appeared to zone out. His eyes were fixed on the car but I could tell he wasn't looking at it anymore. His mind was elsewhere. So I decided to bring him back to life by checking his mental temperature.

I took a deep breath and said, "You know what, I'm sorry I even brought this too you. I know you got a lot going on right now. This my fault."

He blinked a few times and looked at me. "Your fault? How you figure?"

"Because I had no business messing with her husband. If you were married to me I don't know what limits I would go through to protect what was mine, Devin. You are her husband and what we are doing is wrong."

"Go 'head with that shit," he said waving me off. "I don't feel like hearing that right now."

"It's not about what you feel like hearing. It's about what's right." I exhaled like it was the hardest thing I ever had to say to him. "I think we should stop seeing each other, Devin. I don't feel safe and it's obvious that you can't protect me. Go back to your family."

"So what, you not gonna let me see my son?"

I frowned. "Even if I never talked to you again I would never stop you from seeing your son. I don't play that chicken head shit. I want my son to have everything he's due and that includes love from both of his parents." I paused. "I'm saying that I can't see you in that way anymore. You're free to build a relationship with your son but it's over between us."

He glared at me as if he wanted to take my life. "Come on, Clever. You know you don't want it like that. And you better stop saying that shit before I take you up on your offer."

"I'm serious," I paused and pointed to the damage of my car. "This kind of shit is not me. I don't do well with bitches touching my property." I walked closer to him and took my car keys out of his hand. "I care about you but this kind of thing is too draining. I think it's time for me to move on with my life." I reached up and touched the side of his face. "I will always love you, Devin. Goodbye." I activated my alarm system and walked into the house.

I was sitting in the living room playing with Village. I can't believe how much he looks like his father. The way his little face lit up every time he saw mine made me feel warm inside. I was so busy getting revenge on Devin that sometimes I forget that he gave me this beautiful little boy, who was in his image.

I was starting to think that I was going too far with trying to ruin Devin's marriage. When he examined my car yesterday and had it taken to the body shop to be repaired I could tell he felt bad for something he thought his wife did. The way he looked down at me broke my heart. It looked as if he really loved me.

Is it possible for a man to love two women at the same time?

After he examined my car he knocked on the door and gave my aunt two stacks so that I could rent something comfortable until my car was fixed. He went all out and although I wanted him to feel the pain for how he treated me why was my heart so heavy?

"Why you sitting over there looking all crazy?" my aunt asked as she walked into the living room and sat on the other end of the sofa. "You winning yet you could never tell by looking at your face."

I shrugged. "Just thinking." I rubbed my baby's cheek and looked out of the window at nothing.

"Are you thinking 'bout that nigga?" she asked with an attitude. "Again?"

I sighed. "What if I am?"

"Then you's about a dumb bitch." She had no filters with her mouth play. "You got me over here giving you all of my game but you don't appreciate it. If you was going to be doing all this pouting you should've just stayed with the nigga and let him treat you how he wanted."

"So I'm a dumb bitch because I feel bad that the father of my son feels guilty for something I did to my own car?" I put Village on the floor so he could play on his stomach.

"That's not guilt, Clever. What you see is him being scared that he made his own bed and now it's time to lie in it. Think about it for a minute. What do you think bothers him the most? The fact that his wife scratched your car or that his wife knows for a fact that ya'll are fucking?"

"Probably both."

"It ain't about it being both. Which do you think bothers him the most?"

I sighed tiring of this game. "I don't know, Auntie."

"Well I'll tell you since class is in session. The only thing his selfish ass cares about is how much drama he's going to get from his wife. In his mind she knows he is still checking for you. But if my game is tight enough he'll leave his wife and when he does that's when you crush his ass."

"What do you mean by your game being tight?" I asked with a hung jaw. "I'm the one putting in the work."

She laughed hysterically. "My dear niece, you ain't nothing but a puppet in my regime." She paused. I was angry and she must've known because she said, "Don't get mad. If I know my skills the way I think I do in the end he will be on his knees and then you can decide what to do with him."

"He's not leaving his wife," I said although I was hopeful.

She laughed heavily. "Trust me, he will leave his wife. Especially if you activate the entire plan we discussed. You have to make him doubt her. Make him not trust her. You do that and he will leave."

I thought about why she was so interested in doing this. My auntie was married to a man named Marvin for ten years. He was her everything. He was a construction worker at a large agency in Baltimore. He worked hard, bought my auntie anything she wanted and when he was promoted he left her for a white girl. She never recovered from the divorce or the public humiliation. She went from living in a half a million-dollar home to an apartment in the projects.

"Devin is not Marvin, auntie."

The smirk she had on her face washed away. "Never said he was," she frowned. "But he is a man and all of them can be brought to their knees."

When there was loud beeping outside I got on my knees and looked out of the window again. My aunt must've been curious because she looked out of the window too. My eyes flapped a few times when I saw a white Benz with a bow sitting on the top in front of my building. When the driver stepped out and I saw it was Devin raising his hands up to his sides my heart beat paced.

134   *By Shay Hunter*

With my jaw hung I looked over at my auntie.

"Now will you believe me?" she asked.

Not only do I believe her, I will never doubt another thing she tells me.

I am officially sold!

CHAPTER ELEVEN
RAIN

With tear filled eyes I was sitting in my car looking up at that bitch's apartment. I didn't know what car she drove and I was tempted to break every window in the hopes that she would come out. Ever since Devin and me had that argument I was an emotional wreck. I couldn't believe the condition of my life.

The condition of my marriage.

Earlier today I made up with my best friend Jonie and my cousin. I realized with everything going on I couldn't do it without them. But even though she gave me a pep talk I was still confused.

Wanting some answers I pulled the cell phone out of my pocket and dialed a number. My heart danced

By Shay Hunter

around in my chest as I waited for my call to be answered. "Hello," Clever said. I could tell she had a smile on her face. Why was she so fucking happy?

"Are you satisfied?" I asked her. "Because it sounds like you're really happy with yourself."

She laughed a little and asked, "This must be Mrs. Devin?" she giggled. "Now what are you asking me am I happy about?"

The calm sound of her voice made me feel like shit. I hated this bitch more than I realized. She stole my life and it seemed as if it was too easy for her. "Are you satisfied that you came into my life and ruined a happy home?"

"Rain, why don't you realize that happy homes can't be ruined? Only the confused and fucked up ones are up for grabs." She paused. "But try not to take it personal. If it wasn't your husband it would be someone else's."

Tears rolled down my face and hung on my chin. I wiped them off roughly. "They have a special place for women like you. Do you know where it is?"

"Hell," she giggled.

"And you're proud of that? You're proud that Devin used you for your body and when he's done he's going to throw you away?"

"You don't really believe that," she said. "Let's be real. Because if you did believe that you wouldn't be calling me right now." She paused. "I'm a very real threat for you, Rain and I should be."

"I not only believe what you said I'll also tell you this. It's just a matter of time before he breaks your heart. And when he does we'll go out together and get some drinks so you can tell me all about it." I paused. "I wouldn't miss it for anything in the world."

"You see that's where you're wrong. He can't break my heart because I won't allow him. Devin and I have an understanding, Rain," she continued sarcastically. "If anything I'm an instrumental part of your relationship and you should try a little harder to give me that respect."

"Respect?" I yelled. "You don't deserve any fucking respect! You're a washed up whore who can't keep a man of her own so she has to move on other peoples. I will give you a lot of things but respect will never be one of them."

"You talking a lot of shit and yet your voice sounds so unsure."

I swallowed and wiped my tears away again. "Tell me something, Clever. How does it feel to have a son by a man who will never acknowledge him in public?"

Silence.

"I knew that would get you," I continued. Although her silence answered my question about the baby being his son, the vindication was short lived. I now knew something I didn't want to be true. That my husband had a child outside of our marriage.

"Answer me this question," she said. "Did that make you feel better or worse? To learn that the man you chose to spend the rest of your life with has a beautiful boy child by his side chick?"

My body trembled. "You are so evil."

"How am I evil?" she yelled losing the composure she had earlier. "I'm sick of fake ass wives calling me about their fucking husbands. At the end of the day I didn't have a commitment with you. He did. If he was doing so right then you wouldn't need to call me. All would be well in your world but it's not is it?"

"When I find you I am going to kill you."

She hung up.

I placed my cell phone in my purse. I knew in that moment that no matter what I would not stop until I felt her blood between my fingertips.

140   *By Shay Hunter*

CHAPTER TWELVE
CLEVER

See at first my plot for revenge was all about Devin. But since his fake ass wife called I decided to turn things up a notch. Now she was going to experience my wrath in a way that wasn't in the plans. As I pressed the gas heavily toward my destination my phone rang. I hit the answer button and the speakers in my car lit up with Vanessa's voice. "Bitch, when am I going to see you?"

I shook my head and laughed a little. "Oh now you wanna see a bitch."

"Just because I'm not a fan of this little revenge mission of yours doesn't mean that I don't want to see you. You could at least called us so we could come kick it over your new crib."

I blushed because I didn't even know she heard about it. Devin not only stepped up and bought me a new Benz, he also put me in a beautiful condo overlooking the Baltimore Harbor. He was really proving to me that he wanted to be with me and I was surprised at how much attention he was giving me. The way he left my apartment that day I figured I was nonessential. A bitch that could be replaced.

I guess not.

I rolled my eyes and flipped the switch to turn my blinkers on so I could get over in traffic. "I don't feel like hearing a lecture from you right now. So if you calling to tell me why what I'm doing to Devin is wrong than save your voice for someone who wants to hear you sing. Besides, my mind is made up on this end."

"Can I ask you something? Do you feel even a little guilty about what you doing?"

I widened my eyes. "Fuck you talking about? Just because I'm sending the nigga through the loop a little don't mean when I'm done he won't be alright. Besides, after my little plan he'll belong to me anyway. I just want him on his knees first."

"First off that ain't happening. The man ain't leaving his wife even if he's gone. You and me both know that. But even if he did why would you want him? He's the worst, Clever. And you will always be looking over your shoulders wondering if he'll do the same thing to you next. Don't you see that? What kind of man has a baby by his side chick outside of his marriage?"

Click.

I hung up on her ass because she was saying the same shit. Her and Tracy, but I fucked with Tracy the most because she was more like me. We both understood that sometimes you had to teach niggas how to treat you. Tracy and I were so close that we even fucked the same dudes at one point and didn't miss a night's sleep over it. But Vanessa...she was like the nerd who managed to get in with the "In Crowd" and didn't know what to do with us.

When I made it to my destination I pulled my car to the right next to the curb, parked, hopped out and stomped toward the steps leading to Crisp's house.

Crisp's tall body was blocking my view but I knew Devin was there. The moment I made my way around Crisp I saw Devin sitting next to some cute redbone with a wide smile. I stumbled a little not expecting to see him so close to another woman, before getting myself together.

I had a plan and I needed to remember it although what Vanessa just said about him not leaving his wife and doing the same thing to me was still fresh in my mind. I mean was he buying this red bitch a car too?

Instead of confronting him being with another bitch I grabbed my cell phone out of my pocket and flashed it in his face. "You better get your fucking wife before I kill the bitch!"

The redbone hopped up, rushed up the steps and ran through the building's door. I guess she could tell I was mad and wanted to get as far away from me as possible. Good choice. Because I could feel my skin heating up even more when I saw the ass she was toting. It may not have been as fat as mine but it was cute enough for her body type.

Devin stood up, yanked me by my elbow and rushed me to the side of his truck. When we were there he pushed my back against it and frowned at me. "My wife don't even come at me like that when I'm on the block! Fuck wrong with you, son?"

"Son?" I repeated. "Nigga, I'm not your fucking son!" I pushed him away roughly, mostly because I was scared of him hitting me. I can't remember him being this mad before so it had me double thinking myself. Maybe he was getting tired of me after all. "And for your information what's wrong with me is that I can't go a day without your wife calling me! Or harassing me! I mean damn, Devin, don't you got control of your bitch? You a fucking man."

"You damn right I'm a man!"

"Well do something about it! Get your fucking wife before I hurt her feelings!"

He stepped back, wiped his hand over his face and looked up at the sky. I could tell that he was mad but this part was necessary for the build up. "What did you say when she called?"

"I said I wasn't fucking with her husband. That I never have but she wouldn't hear it. She started threatening my life and some more shit."

He walked up to me and kissed me on the forehead. "Alright, ma. I'll talk to her. Tell her to stop messing with my man's girl."

"You know she don't believe that shit no more after she saw the pictures."

"It don't matter what she believes. It matters what I tell her."

"Thank you," I said as if that was the only reason I came by and I didn't want to see him. "I'll get up with you later." I walked around him and toward my car a few spaces behind his truck. I didn't get five steps away before he yanked me back.

"So you gonna leave a nigga like that?"

"How am I leaving you?" I frowned.

"You came over here and fucked my head up and then you 'bout to bounce?"

I rolled my eyes. "Devin, I know you working. I was just coming by to tell you about your wife because lately her threats have been getting a little strange. I didn't mean to stop your hustle. You're free to do you."

I don't remember the last time I saw his face contort like that. I couldn't tell if he wanted to fuck me or kill me. I got my answer when I was suddenly in the back of his truck riding his dick. Although it was feeling good there was another reason I went with him so easily.

I continued to buck my hips and when I saw it got to feeling really good to him I hit the button on my cell phone that was hanging out of my purse. I waited a few seconds and through the moans I could hear his wife say hello. I moaned louder to conceal her voice from him and then I said, "Devin, you feel so good."

"This pussy so wet, bay," he whispered as he dug deeper into me.

His voice wasn't as loud as I wanted so I moved my hips harder and wider. When his head dropped back I said, "I'm so scared, baby. Scared you're going to leave me again."

"Don't…uh…damn, ma, this pussy is so tight."

"Devin, do you hear me?" I said as I slowed up a little, controlling his orgasm in the process. "I'm afraid you gonna leave me."

"Fuck, Clever!" he yelled out of apparent frustration. "Why would I leave you when I love you?" he paused. "Now stop fucking around and give me that pussy."

Having heard what I wanted her to hear I fucked him harder. Although he was consumed with the sound of me moaning in his ear, I was consumed with his wife weeping loudly from my cell phone.

Checkmate.

CHAPTER THIRTEEN
DEVIN

Rain was hysterical. She had me pinned up in the corner as she took swings in my direction with a knife in her hand. This was the second time she pulled this shit and I told her there wouldn't be another time. Had I known she would be on some wild shit I would never have come home.

I fuck with Clever hard. Shawty feels and looks exactly how I like my bitches to look. But this last move was messy on her part. She claimed the phone accidently dialed Rain when we were fucking in my truck since Rain was the last person to call her phone, but I don't believe her. I was going to have another conversation with her later about this shit but first I had to get out of this situation.

By Shay Hunter

"Baby, can you listen to me?" I yelled as I backed into the corner trying to figure out how I was going to get out of this alive. With my eyes on the shiny blade I calmly said, "I didn't fuck that girl." I looked into her red eyes and back at the knife. "I don't know what you think but it ain't happen with me."

"I know you were with her!" she screamed as she continued to thrust the knife in my direction. "I heard your fucking voice! I know it was you!"

"How it's gonna be me when I been with Prize and Mace all day? You probably heard Crisp, Rain. Call him up now if you don't believe me."

"Why so I can listen at him lie like you trained him to?" she yelled. When she took a chance to wipe the tears away with her wrist I smacked her so hard in the face she fell backwards. The knife went spinning out of her hand a few feet away from her.

Since she was disarmed I stomped toward the knife and crawled over top of her. With all of my weight on her body I placed the knife against her throat. "Now how the fuck you feel huh?" I backhanded her in the face with the other hand while I maintained control of the knife. "Didn't I tell you what would happen if you pointed another knife at me?" I smacked her again. "Huh?"

"Get off of me, mothafucka!" she screamed while trying to get from up under me. "I hate you!"

"You hate me?" I yelled as I lowered my head and screamed in her face. "Is that how you really feel?"

"I fucking hate you, you dirty dick nigga! The only person you care about is that bitch! You violating and you gonna pay for this shit too, Devin! I promise!"

I know I should feel more sympathetic since I was fucking shawty but I was angry that she acted like I never did shit for her in life. It was because of me and all the nights I hustled that she was able to go to college. It was because of me that she didn't live in the projects anymore but a fly ass crib in Georgetown. So what I fucked a bitch or two? I never made her feel like she wasn't in first place.

I was done with this shit.

Since my back was sweating from moving around so much I stood up, tossed the knife in the sink and walked back over to her. Looking down at her I said, "I'ma be one hundred with you. I'm a nigga and sometimes I feel the need to have a little variety. At least you know who she is now. If anything you should be happy because without her I don't think we would make it."

My wife's beautiful chocolate complexion turned beet red. "I can't believe you just said that shit to me."

"I'm tired of lying to you, Rain. I'm tired of playing games with you when I know I'm not gonna change.

But I can promise you this, if you can get with this program and understand that I will never put another bitch before you then we gonna be alright."

For some reason it felt like a ton of bricks had been lifted off me. Although she wasn't happy about it in the moment I felt relieved. I was tired of lying to her and I didn't see me getting rid of Clever any time soon. And at some point Rain was going to have to be real. There wasn't another nigga alive who would treat her the way I did. If she acted right and stopped tripping it was a win-win for everybody.

My wife was sexy as shit but she was boring and that's where Clever came in. If Rain wasn't talking about the bitches at her school and how they were so jealous of her, or the professors who loved her so much for picking up on the lessons quick, she was studying.

"I will never forgive you for how you're treating me right now, Devin." She wiped tears off of her face with the sleeve of her sweatshirt. "Never." She stood up and grabbed the knife out of the sink. I hopped away from her thinking she was coming at me again. Instead she snatched her keys from the table and her purse from the couch before she walked out the door.

I didn't know where she was going but I knew I didn't feel like chasing her either. If she wanted to do something stupid then it would be her fault.

Instead of running back on the streets right away I turned around and looked at my condo. I imagined I was a bachelor who didn't have to put up with any of the emotional shit. I walked around the living room and then moved in the direction of the bedroom.

The bed was made and I hung in the doorway and looked at it. Everything was neat and it smelled good as usual. Rain may have been mad but when it came to cleaning the house she didn't play. She left nothing out when it came to cooking for me or keeping a clean home. The moment I realized that I knew if I was single I would never have a crib this put together.

I'd probably have sheets for curtains instead of the velvet burgundy ones hanging on the windows. I'd probably be sleeping on the mattress because I'd be too busy to make the bed or care about shit like this. I don't want to even think about how clean it would be. I could see shit all over the place and I probably wouldn't bring any bitch I was serious about here.

I shook my head, took off my clothes and grabbed a shower. When I was done I borrowed some of my wife's Jergins lotion and smoothed it over my body. Then I slid in some fresh boxers and a white t-shirt, grabbed a bag of cheese Doritos, my favorite, from the counter. I chewed a few chips and wanted to take a nap because it was the end of the month and the first was approaching. Since that's when I made most of my money I needed to make sure all of my soldiers had work. But before going to sleep I locked the bedroom door. I wasn't about to wake up with my wife hanging over my body with a knife again.

When I was comfortable I crawled on top of the comforter without pulling the sheets back, something Rain hated, and went to sleep.

I thought I was dreaming when I heard my phone ringing repeatedly. I raised my head, looked at the clock and then reached for my phone. It was about 9 o'clock at night, six hours after my wife and me got into a fight. I guess I was more tired than I realized because a nap almost turned into going to sleep for the night.

I reached for my cell phone and saw it was Clever. At first I thought she wanted me to come over but lately that hadn't been the case. If I didn't say I wanted to see her she wouldn't suggest it. And that was cool with me just as long as when I made the call the pussy was open and she was there. Pressing the phone against my ear I yawned and said, "What up, sexy?"

"What up?" she screamed. "What's up is that bitch of yours and her little friends tried to jump me! I'm at the hospital right now, Devin! Come up here and get me! I'm scared!"

CHAPTER FOURTEEN

CLEVER

"I'm sorry for hitting you that hard," Tracy said as I sat in the emergency room. "But I wanted to make it realistic."

I held an ice pack closely to my eye as I was sitting on the edge of the bed in the hospital. Earlier today I had Tracy come over and bruise me up a little. I asked Vanessa to come over too but as usual she told me about all of the reasons why what I was doing was wrong. Fuck that bitch. She could keep her miserable ass in the house and leave me alone.

"Don't worry about it," I said as I tried to relieve some of the throbbing sensation I was feeling in my face. "I'm just glad you were able to make it concrete.

Because if you didn't he wouldn't believe his wife actually had somebody jump me."

"So what's the plan?"

"Well I told him his wife's people jumped me to make him mad at her."

She frowned a little. "You think that's enough to make him leave her? Or be mad at her? Because his wife fought the side chick."

"I know he'll be mad. But more than anything my aunt said he'll be irritated." I giggled. "That he'll probably say fuck everything just to get out of the situation."

"How do you know it will work?"

"Because if he didn't care about me he would've left me alone. Instead this nigga bought me a car and a condo." I paused. "He can't leave me. But his actions are showing he can leave her."

She shook her head. "How did she even get your number?"

"I think she got it off of the cell phone bill." I shrugged. "Who knows?"

"Dudes be slipping these days like shit. They better get up extra early in the morning if they want to hide a side bitch from their wives."

"Tell me about it." When I saw Devin walking down the hall and toward me I said, "But look, he on his way back here. I'll get up with you later."

"Work it, bitch," she whispered before wiggling away. "Bye, Devin," she said as she walked past him.

The moment he moved closer to me I laid it on thick with a little moaning. He walked up to me and wrapped his arms around me without even saying anything. A few seconds later he separated from me and looked down at my face. Raising my chin a little he said, "Bay, why did you call that girl and let her hear us fucking in the truck?"

Although he was asking me a question I was grinning inside because he said *'that girl'* instead of *'his wife'*. "What you talking about?" I asked trying to play it off. "I told you it was an accident. Why you keep coming at me like that?"

"Me and my wife got into a fight today behind a that call."

That shit was short lived. I guess he couldn't wait to say wife again.

"She almost tried to stab me. Why would you do that? I know it was on purpose."

Salty about the way he said my wife when he knew how it made me feel I laid into him. "First the fuck of all you should be asking me how I feel instead of coming at me about an accident where you were not the victim. Don't forget that it was your idea to have sex in the truck remember? I was trying to go home and you pulled me back. Not to mention that your precious wife called to harass me earlier that day. Had she not, her number would not have been on my phone to be pushed accidently." I paused. "So excuse me if I regain the focus again. And that is that your wife and her little friends tried to kill me."

"Did she have a knife?" he asked with lowered brows.

I thought his question was weird but I went with it. "Yeah. Why?"

He sighed. "Where did she do it?"

"At my old spot."

"I don't want you going back to that place again."

"My aunt is there. And she watches our son sometimes there."

"I don't want you at that fucking spot no more and definitely not with my son.

Hoetic Justice   163

"But I'm gonna be cool," I said knowing it was probably annoying.

"Look at your face, bay," he said in a compassionate tone. He exhaled heavily. "It's a lot going on right now and until I figure out what I want to do I'd feel better if you wouldn't go back. If your aunt wants to watch Village over my crib she can. Just don't go back over there."

"I can't just leave the place forever, Devin. It took me forever to get that lease. My rent is only $75.00 a month because of Village."

He laughed at me. "How 'bout I pay off your lease for two years at that place and you just stay at your condo?"

I tried to suppress my grin but it wasn't working. The wounds on my face ached. "If you say so." I paused. "I ain't gonna fight with you." I touched the top of his hand. "So what you doing tonight?"

"It's the first so I gotta go handle business. Don't worry about packing up the rest of your shit at your old spot. I'll have someone do all of that. Just take my son and don't go back over there."

"Why?"

"Because I'm not sure what she might do."

CHAPTER FIFTEEN
DEVIN

I was sitting in the passenger seat of a rental talking to my wife on the phone. My little homie Crisp was driving. The more I heard her voice the more irritated I grew. I started not to answer the phone but I knew I wasn't coming home tonight and I didn't want her blowing up my phone when I was with Clever.

I was taking shawty to a nice hotel to try to make up for what Rain had her friends do to her face. The funny thing is she didn't bother to mention what she did to Clever. It was okay to me because I didn't feel like arguing with her about it anyway. She got one out on my shawty and now she was either going to have to get herself together or step off.

By Shay Hunter

"So you gonna go be up under that bitch all night? Is that why you telling me you not coming home, Devin?"

Frustrated I closed my eyes and pressed the phone closer to my ear. "I told you how I felt about the matter. I love you, Rain. You're my wife. But our marriage is boring at best. Let me have a little fun so that I can hang around more."

I heard Crisp chuckle but when I threw him an evil glare he covered his mouth with his hand and then wiped the smile off of his face. I wasn't trying to play my wife in front of anybody but I had to be real with her too. But the little homie was out of line for laughing.

"If you hate me so much why would you even marry me?" Rain asked bringing my attention back on her. "Just answer me that."

I sighed. "Never said I hated you."

"That's how you make me feel."

"Fuck! What you want me to say? I love you, Rain, but I'm not about to lie to you no more either. You're my wife and if you want to stay that way I want to have you. But shawty gonna be around too."

"You are going to pay for this shit."

"So you threatening me again? Even after I warned you about that shit?"

"I'm stating a fact, Devin." She sniffled. "You're going to pay for this shit."

I laughed because her threats held no weight. She kept saying what she was going to do to me and in the end she was still here. So if she wanted out she could go at anytime and my rent would still be paid and my dick would still get sucked. "You do what you gotta do. I'm not about to—"

When I saw an unmarked white car flash its lights behind us my heart kicked up thunder. I hung up on

Rain without an explanation. I had twenty thousand dollars worth of cocaine in the trunk that Crisp was going to drop off to the soldiers when he took me to Prize and Mace's crib. But now it looked like I'd never get there.

"Fuck, what should I do?" Crisp asked as his eyes alternated from the rearview mirror to the road. "Want me to gun it?"

As much as I wanted to say yes I knew that shit could get worse. I was hoping that we were being pulled over for some dumb shit but I couldn't be sure. "Were you speeding?"

His eyes widened as he looked at me with confusion. "Naw, man. You in here with me. You felt how fast I was driving."

He was right. But I also knew Rain dominated my attention so anything could've been the case. He could've been going ninety miles and hour and as mad as I was I would not have known. "Pull over, man."

"What about the brick?"

"Guess we gotta deal with it."

I was sitting in my living room of my condo with my elbows on my knees. My hands were clasped in front of me and my right leg was shaking. I knew Rain was mad but I never expected her to go this far. Had it not been for Crisp swearing that the package was his I might have been in jail longer than a few days. I knew he was a loyal little dude but I had intentions on doing him right once this shit was all said and done. But first I had to deal with my wife.

The moment she came in the house she seemed shocked to see me. I unclasped my hands, stood up and walked over to her. When I was in her face I came down on her jaw with a closed fist like she was a man. Since she didn't give a fuck about my life and had me arrested I didn't care about hers. She was the only one that knew I was going with Crisp to pick up work. She knew everything about my routine.

On the floor, with a bloodied mouth and red teeth she broke out crying.

"I knew you had everything to do with that shit, bitch. And I never thought you would stoop so low."

"Devin, I swear on everything I love, that she's lying. Why would I call the cops on you? Think about it, baby! She want's my marriage! She wants my life!"

"When I come back home I want you and your shit out of here," I said before grabbing my keys.

"Devin, nooooo!" she yelled as I closed the door. I could still hear her screaming my name as I stomped to my car.

I was in my ride on my way to Prize's house. My knuckles still throbbed from hitting my wife and instead of feeling sympathy I was madder than ever. When my phone rang I answered it without checking the caller ID. "Hey, Devin," Clever said to me. "How you doing?"

"Not good, ma."

She sighed. "I'm so sorry about what you been through the last few days. I can't believe your wife would go so far to get back at you although I can say that I'm not surprised." She paused. "So what you gonna do?"

"I gotta figure some shit out. In the meantime I'll be staying at your crib for a little while." I turned on my friends' street and parked. "That is if it's okay with you?"

"You know I got you, bay. You don't even have to ask."

I liked how she tried to sound hardcore. Like she wasn't glad a nigga was going to be living with her for a little while. It was cute. "Aight, mami. I'll see you in a bit."

"Wait, before you hang up I'm at the store. You want me to bring you anything?"

"Yeah. Grab me a pack of Black N Mild's and some cheese Doritos."

"Got you," she said in a seductive tone. "You got the key so when you get there go straight to my room.

Don't even worry about washing up. I'll take care of that for you too."

I chuckled. "No doubt."

CHAPTER SIXTEEN

CLEVER

After getting off the phone with Devin I tried to hide my smile but my auntie wasn't having it. "So you finally got what you wanted," she said to me as she puffed on a cigarette and blew the smoke in the air. I hated those things but since Village was over Vanessa's house I didn't see a problem with it.

"If that's what you want to call it," I grinned.

She looked at me and dropped her jaw. "What you mean if that's what I call it? Let's recap everything that went down."

"I'm not fucking with you."

"Seriously," she continued. "Before I got in the picture you were getting the occasional dick down from your boy. But after I got into the picture *and* you agreed to stick to my plan you got a new car, a new apartment and the man. If anything you should be on your knees kissing my feet. Luckily for you I have on shoes."

I rolled my eyes. "I won't do all of that but I will give you your props. Had it not been for you I wouldn't have it so sweet."

"Good, now it's time to finish what you started. My friend's nephew is ready to put a bullet in his head like we talked about. He knows where he hangs out and all you have to do is give the word."

"Auntie, I don't know if I want to go that far anymore. I mean, he bought me a car, a condo and left his wife. I don't know if I want to have him killed now."

By Shay Hunter

She frowned and seemed irritated. "What if I tell you it's too late and that things are already I motion? What would you say then?"

When she said that my heart thumped. Originally the plan was to run his pockets, get him locked up and then killed in prison. And before taking his life they were going to show him my picture. But now I want to make things work. "Auntie, I'm begging you, please let me handle this." I turned my head so that she could look in my eyes. "I really appreciate everything that you did but it's over now. Okay?"

"Is he what you really want?" she asked smashing the cigarette in the ashtray.

"I don't know what I want. I just know that I love spending time with him and I don't want him dead." I looked over at her because I could tell by her stone expression that she didn't approve. "Will you let me?"

"I don't know, niece. I'll see if I can call them boys off." She sighed. "At the end of the day I just want you to be happy."

I was shocked because she never talked to me like that before. "Whoa…what did I do to deserve that?"

"I'm serious. I give you a hard time but you remind me of your mother before she died. She was my little sister and I was overprotective of her too. Just remember something, sometimes the cake is not as sweet as it looks."

"What happened to that power strength thing you were talking about?"

"I was right about that. Since you were able to pull him from his wife your power strength is pretty strong. Just be careful about the vision you have in your mind about him, Clever. Your mother gave you your name for a reason. She wanted you to always be smart, to always use your head. His kind does not change and if

he hurts you again the nigga is dead."

CHAPTER SEVENTEEN
RAIN

So many tears covered my eyes as I sped down the highway that I could barely see. My life felt as if it was crashing down around me. I can't believe after all of the years we were married that he would actually play me like this. Like I was a nobody. He promised to love and protect me forever but he lied.

I was just about to drive my car off of the end of a bridge when I looked to my right and saw Clever walking into a convenience store. At first I couldn't believe my eyes but when I leaned to the right I saw it really was her I whipped my ride over and parked away from her car. My pressure went higher when I

By Shay Hunter

saw it was a Benz. Devin probably bought her that shit too.

When I peaked a little I saw her aunt was sitting in the car. I didn't feel like dealing with her because I needed to have a conversation with Clever and wasn't nothing going to stop me.

I don't know what made me take the knife out of my house awhile back but I did. I kept it in the glove compartment. As if I knew this moment would always come. Since I had it with me I decided to use it. With the knife in my palm I tucked the handle in my jeans and pulled my shirt over top of it. I tiptoed in the store while Clever's aunt was looking at her phone.

When I got inside Clever was standing next to the Doritos aisle, picking up a large bag of chips. This didn't do anything but make me angrier because I knew she was buying them for him. Doritos were Devin's favorite. Before she walked to the cashier I quickly stepped in her direction and said, "So how does it feel now that you got everything you wanted? Are you happy?"

She turned around and her eyes widened as if she saw a ghost. She tried to wave me off with her hand. "You know what I'm not going to even argue with you. We had our thing and now it's over. Just leave it alone."

She turned her back on me and I pushed her. She stumbled a few feet and faced me again. "Fuck you, slut! Don't tell me what to do!"

"You know what at first I wasn't going to hurt your feelings but you asked for it," she said waving her finger in my face. "You stepping at me like I'm your fucking husband! You should work a little better on your game or you would've kept him!"

"I won't let you keep him," I said as I balled my fists up. "Do you hear me?"

By Shay Hunter

She laughed at me and I felt my blood boiling. "Do you realize how ridiculous you sound? I already got the nigga."

"He doesn't want to be with me because you lied! Somehow you knew he was going to be taking a package and you called the cops on him."

She smirked. "I sure did. It's amazing how cheap your so called best friend go's for. Apparently you've been talking to her a little too much and for a few bucks she told me everything she knew about Devin, including his drop offs."

I was so angry I was trembling. I knew I should've cut Jonie's fake ass off and now I was paying for it.

"So do yourself a favor," she continued, "Stop preaching to the side chick. Why don't you go on somewhere and call your cousin and them."

"You are the lowest type of bitch in the world and I hope he does to you exactly what he's doing to me."

"Why should he do to me what he did to you? You're the boring one not me. You don't like to hang out with him! You don't like to fuck him! You don't even cook decent meals anymore. If anything you practically gave him to me so you need to blame yourself. Unlike you I have intentions on doing whatever I need to do to keep him."

When she moved closer to me her arms moved like they had a mind of their own. She got to scratching and clawing at my face and I could feel blood run down my cheeks. "You stupid, ugly bitch! I hate you for being in his life," she yelled at me as if she was the wife. She continued to scratch at my face and although I tried to protect myself it wasn't working. I took each blow. "He belongs to me!"

When she said those things I snapped. I removed the kitchen knife from my pants and dashed toward her. By the time I wanted to take back the jab it was too late. I successfully stabbed her into the stomach.

Her eyes spread as she fell back into the chips. She looked up at me with pitiful eyes.

"If I can't have my husband nobody will!"

EPILOGUE
ONE MONTH LATER

A month after the stabbing Clever was finally able to walk around. Although she needed to take it easy she celebrated by getting up early and cooking breakfast for her family.

Devin tried to reason with her and to get her to rest. He said he would cook for everyone like he had been but Clever was adamant about serving him. In her mind had Rain did the same thing he wouldn't be sitting at her kitchen table with his son. Clever was determined to do everything Rain didn't even though the knife pierced her intestinal wall.

When everything was prepared she scooped the food on Devin's plate and fed Village before putting him to bed. Her aunt said she'd come over later to pick

By Shay Hunter

him up so that she and Devin could have some alone time. Especially since her niece was feeling better.

A lot changed in Clever's world. In the month following the stabbing Rain was arrested but was able to post her bond pending the trial. She did major damage to Clever's intestinal wall when she stabbed her and was facing some serious time if convicted. With the trial in two months she was worried about her freedom.

"Baby, I'm going to take a bath," Clever said to him.

"You sure? It's too early to be getting down in the tub," he said while sitting on the sofa.

"I'm fine, Devin. I'll be back when I'm done."

"Okay, and when you finish getting dressed come back out in the living room. So I can beat that ass in Madden."

"Like you can really fuck with me," Clever giggled.

Hoetic Justice   187

"We'll see about that."

Clever laughed and walked to her room. When she got there her cell phone rang a few times. Since her friends and aunt called the house phone she had no idea who it was. In a great mood she picked it up and said, "Hello."

Instead of receiving a greeting she heard, *'I know this is fucked up, baby. But I gotta stay with this bitch so that she doesn't press charges. But I swear to God when this case is over I'm coming back home. I love you'.*

The voice belonged to Devin and she knew he was talking to his wife.

Clever didn't realize she was crying until a large tear plopped on her knee. The phone remained pressed against her ear until she heard, "Congratulations on winning, Clever," Rain said in a soft voice. "But now I'm the side chick. Good luck with keeping him."

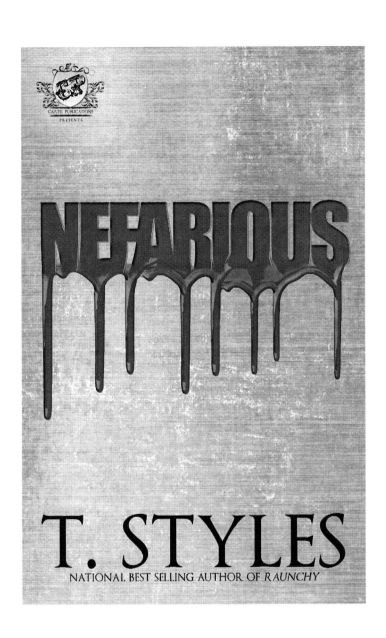

CARTEL PUBLICATIONS
PRESENTS

NEFARIOUS

T. STYLES

NATIONAL BEST SELLING AUTHOR OF *RAUNCHY*

The Cartel Publications Order Form
www.thecartelpublications.com
Inmates **ONLY** receive novels for $10.00 per book.
(Mail Order **MUST** come from inmate directly to receive discount)

Shyt List 1	_____	$15.00
Shyt List 2	_____	$15.00
Shyt List 3	_____	$15.00
Shyt List 4	_____	$15.00
Shyt List 5	_____	$15.00
Pitbulls In A Skirt	_____	$15.00
Pitbulls In A Skirt 2	_____	$15.00
Pitbulls In A Skirt 3	_____	$15.00
Pitbulls In A Skirt 4	_____	$15.00
Victoria's Secret	_____	$15.00
Poison 1	_____	$15.00
Poison 2	_____	$15.00
Hell Razor Honeys	_____	$15.00
Hell Razor Honeys 2	_____	$15.00
A Hustler's Son 2	_____	$15.00
Black and Ugly	_____	$15.00
Black and Ugly As Ever	_____	$15.00
Year Of The Crackmom	_____	$15.00
Deadheads	_____	$15.00
The Face That Launched A	_____	$15.00
Thousand Bullets		
The Unusual Suspects	_____	$15.00
Miss Wayne & The Queens of DC	_____	$15.00
Paid In Blood (eBook Only)	_____	$15.00
Raunchy	_____	$15.00
Raunchy 2	_____	$15.00
Raunchy 3	_____	$15.00
Mad Maxxx	_____	$15.00
Quita's Dayscare Center	_____	$15.00
Quita's Dayscare Center 2	_____	$15.00
Pretty Kings	_____	$15.00
Pretty Kings 2	_____	$15.00
Pretty Kings 3	_____	$15.00
Silence Of The Nine	_____	$15.00
Silence Of The Nine 2	_____	$15.00
Prison Throne	_____	$15.00
Drunk & Hot Girls	_____	$15.00
Hersband Material	_____	$15.00
The End: How To Write A	_____	$15.00
Bestselling Novel In 30 Days (Non-Fiction Guide)		

By Shay Hunter

Upscale Kittens	_____	$15.00
Wake & Bake Boys	_____	$15.00
Young & Dumb	_____	$15.00
Young & Dumb 2:	_____	$15.00
Tranny 911	_____	$15.00
Tranny 911: Dixie's Rise	_____	$15.00
First Comes Love, Then Comes Murder	_____	$15.00
Luxury Tax	_____	$15.00
The Lying King	_____	$15.00
Crazy Kind Of Love	_____	$15.00
And They Call Me God	_____	$15.00
The Ungrateful Bastards	_____	$15.00
Lipstick Dom	_____	$15.00
A School of Dolls	_____	$15.00
KALI: Raunchy Relived	_____	$15.00
Skeezers	_____	$15.00
Hoetic Justice	_____	$15.00

Please add $4.00 **PER BOOK** for shipping and handling.

The Cartel Publications * P.O. BOX 486 OWINGS MILLS MD 21117

Name: _____

Address: _____

City/State: _____

Contact# & Email:

_____

Please allow 5-7 BUSINESS days before shipping.

The Cartel Publications is NOT responsible for prison orders rejected.

NO PERSONAL CHECKS ACCEPTED

STAMPS NO LONGER ACCEPTED

Hoetic Justice   191

CPSIA information can be obtained at www.ICGtesting.com
Printed in the USA
LVOW08s1813130516

488143LV00001B/121/P